Temp

by David Cook

Also by David Cook

The Soldier Chronicles novella series
Liberty or Death
Heart of Oak
Blood on the Snow
Marksman
Death is a Duty

Fire and Steel: The Soldier Chronicles Books 1-5

Battle Scars: A Collection of Short Stories Volume I

Poems for the Forlorn

04/20/99 - An account of the Columbine High School massacre

A'r holl wlad i gyd yn codi
Â'u hen arfau gyda'i gily',
A'u pladuriau, a'u ffyn ddwybig,
A'r crymanau, i gymeryd.

And the whole country rising up
together, with their ancient arms,
and their scythes and their pitchforks
and the reaping hooks, to seize the enemy.

Ballad by Philip Dafydd

The First Day

Wednesday, 22nd February, 1797

The night was calm and moonlit. Silver touched the limestone and sandstone Pembrokeshire coastline. A small wind came from the glimmering Irish Sea, but it brought no malice.

That was when the warship was sighted a mile off the peninsula near Fishguard, a small fishing village nestled in a valley where the River Gwaun meets the sea. By dawn, when the sky was still grey, the land was grey, and a thin grey mist hovered like fallen wisps of cloud, the ship reached the harbour's anchorage. Six boats were dropped into the cold water and rowed ashore. Redcoats manning a small coastal fort high above the harbour's bluff that over looked Cardigan Bay watched them intently. The stone fortress that protected Fishguard had well-maintained guns, but none of them erupted in warning or threat, because HMS *Britannia* was expected.

Major Mansel Yates of the Fishguard Volunteer Infantry observed the boats approach through the dirty lens of a weather-beaten telescope. 'They are lucky this morning,' he said with a cheerful voice to the two men flanking him. One was a captain with dark eyes and sharp eyebrows, the other was a sergeant with a chest like a blacksmith. 'Lucky indeed,' Yates continued, momentarily staring up at the pearly glow in the sky that indicated where the sun was. *Britannia* was three days late, and Yates had put their delay due to the fierceness of the Irish Sea. 'But then, Colonel Tate was always a fortunate and propitious soul. Did I tell you about the time we ambushed the rebels at Charleston back in '80?'

'Yes, sir,' the captain responded uninterestedly.

They watched the long oars row the vessels closer to shore. Figures in the leading boat were visible at the foredeck and gunwales. They stared back at the coast, where smoke rose from chimneys and lights flickered from houses, warehouses and other trading depots.

'The man's a rogue,' Yates continued of his infatuation, 'but you'll not meet a finer soldier, nor a finer gentleman.'

The captain grunted, thinking the major was talking like a besotted fool.

'Lucky,' Yates repeated. He was in his early forties, of average height, a build more of fat than muscle and had a ruddy-cheeked face. It was a genial face with small, bright blue eyes. He had been an officer of the Volunteers for three years, having been invalided out of the army at the end of the war with the Americans. He returned to his beloved home to help manage his family's estate, which gave him three hundred acres of land when his father died seven years ago. He had been shot in the left arm leaving him with partial feeling and weakness. Despite his wound, he was delighted to be offered the majority.

'Strange colour of their coats, sir?' the sergeant rasped, squinting down at the boats through the smear of light.

'Colour, Sergeant Rosser?' Yates glanced at him and then turned back to the crafts. He adjusted the lens, wiped water from them and then trained the scope for a closer look. 'Dark red, perhaps,' he allowed.

'Looks like dandy grey russet or black to me, sir,' Rosser observed suspiciously.

'We'll soon find out, won't we?' Yates, unable to truly tell because of the haze, smiled in wonderment and snapped shut his glass. The Fishguard Volunteers wore a short red coat faced white with light infantry wings, white breeches and a black slouched hat turned up on the left. A green plume and a white band with the words '*Ich Dien*' German for 'I serve', a motto used by Welsh regiments serving King George III were stitched in black. Yates, like Vickers, wore a thick coat over his scarlet jacket, kidskin gloves and oilskin-coated cocked hats. 'Captain Vickers, with me. Sergeant Rosser, I want you and your section as honour guard.'

Rosser looked blank. 'Honour guard, sir?'

Yates, emollient and softly spoken, smiled again. Moisture on the oilskin gave the hat a silver sheen. 'Of course, sergeant,' he said. 'We have honoured guests to greet.'

'Yes, sir,' Rosser answered but flashed Vickers a sceptical look.

The three men descended the parapet steps and strode back through the courtyard. The two officers then climbed up onto saddled horses and trotted up along the single track, which snaked down the isthmus towards the small port. Delicate threads of fog whirled around the horses' legs as they passed through it.

As the boats' keels scraped aground, the sailors leaped down to steady them and a tall officer wearing a thick grey cloak clasped at his throat gracefully stepped down onto the rushing shore. His tall boots sank into the soft yellow sand, but he managed to stay upright when a wave foamed white and forceful at his feet. Yates and his men were waiting. He went down to meet the newcomer. The Volunteers in their red serge jackets and bright white crossbelts, formed behind, stood rigidly to attention. The two officers saluted each other and, beaming like old friends, clasped each other's hands.

'By God, it's good to see you again, Bill,' Yates said with genuine affection. 'I should rightly be saying, sir.'

Tate dismissed that last comment with an energetic wave of his hand. 'I'll have none of that, Mansel, old friend,' he said with the drawl of South Carolina. 'How long has it been? Twelve years?'

'Fourteen years,' Yates reproached with a firmer grip. The soldiers were disembarking the boats in good order; the bosuns and the sergeants were bellowing orders behind them.

Tate shook his head at the number of years gone by. He was forty-four years old, of slender build, with pale eyes and a long weather-beaten face with a cleft chin. 'Too long for friends not to see each other,' he said, then remembered something. 'You look well. How's your arm?'

Yates was pleased he remembered. 'It goes numb from time to time, and I have never been able to get full use from it, but I was lucky to keep it, so I can't complain.'

'Damned lucky,' Tate agreed.

'How was the journey?'

The American took off his cocked hat, made damp by the mist, and ran a hand through greying hair. 'Dolphins saw us in, there were grey seals on the rocks and Captain Le Haillan thought he saw a whale off the cape,' Tate said, smiling with white teeth. 'I feel like we've already been welcomed.'

Yates laughed and then heard a polite cough from over his shoulder. He half turned to see Vickers waiting keenly to be introduced. 'Of course, my apologies,' the major said, acknowledging his subordinate with a nod. 'Allow me to introduce Captain Dewi Vickers. A most able company commander and one I am extremely proud to have serve with me.'

Vickers gave Tate a sharp salute. 'Major Yates has told me of your gallantry, sir. I am honoured to make your acquaintance.'

Tate seemed awkward with the praise. He fiddled with his hat before placing it back on his head. 'I hope I don't disappoint you, Captain.'

'Not at all, sir,' Vickers said briskly. 'Major Yates often spoke of your capability in dealing with the rebels of that ghastly conflict. Myself, I have not seen action, so it's rewarding to know and converse with those men with experience. I have a great respect for men like you, sir. I hope to learn from you.'

Tate pursed his lips and gave a short nod.

'There is one matter . . .' Vickers's voice trailed away.

'Yes?' Tate said, raising an eyebrow.

Vickers bobbed his head with appreciation at being allowed to continue. 'I was just wondering about your colours, sir.'

'Colours?'

'Your coat and that of your men appear to be dark brown, sir, not regulation red,' Vickers said in a helpful tone.

'You're very perceptive, Captain,' Tate remarked flatly. 'Unfortunately, our coats were supplied incorrectly dyed. The regiment's former colonel still bought them, and we've not been supplied with replacements. However, my men have all regulation necessaries, their muskets have all been oiled and their flints are screwed and well-seated. You'll not see a finer legion. Though I do see a change that will soon allow us to,' he paused briefly, 'transform our colours, as you so adequately put it.' He finished with a charismatic smile.

Vickers wondered why he said '*legion*', but decided not to press the matter for the moment. 'Very good, sir.'

'And now I must insist we share a drink,' Yates implored. 'Your men are welcome to billet at the fort. It's a devil of a trek up, but there is plenty of room. How many men do you have?' He craned to see past Tate.

'Two hundred.'

Yates's cheerfulness flagged. He heard Vickers groan behind. 'We might struggle a little to accommodate. There's a disused farm nearby. The majority of your men can use the granary or share the fields with my men. We have our own tents.'

'My men haven't been issued tents, so we'll use the farm.'

'We are a little thin on the stores, but we have some bread, salted meat and ale.'

'No need to worry yourself,' Tate said cheerfully, 'we have brought our own rations. I've tobacco and a case of fine brandy to share with you and your officers later. I wanted to take my rogues out on a manoeuvre first. We've been at sea too long and need to stretch our legs. I don't want my men to get goddamned soft, and this fine morning will be perfect.'

'Very good,' Yates answered genially.

'Perhaps you will join us?' Tate asked him, though to Vickers it seemed like a demand.

'Much obliged, Bill.'

'Good.' Tate turned, nodded and two of his officers stepped forward. 'This is Captain Le Haillan,' he said, indicating a tall man with pale features and a hint of red hair on his face. The captain immediately gave a smart salute.

'Captain,' Yates said.

'Le Haillan?' Vickers said, frown lines creasing his brow. 'Sounds French.'

There was an embarrassed silence, punctuated by the sounds of Tate's men still disembarking and forming up on the sand. The soldiers wore outdated peaked leather caps with falling horsehair manes, a headdress that light infantry or dragoons wore during the American War of Independence.

Le Haillan's mouth twitched. 'My ancestors,' he said with a crisp English accent, 'were Huguenots.'

Yates coughed to cover his embarrassment at Vickers's impolite question, to which the captain seemed to be oblivious.

Tate glowered. 'This is Lieutenant Marrock, another able officer under my command.'

Marrock was in his early twenties, with chestnut hair and a freckled complexion. With sullen eyes, he flicked his gaze from the Welshmen and up to the village where smoke coursed lazily up from the chimneys to smudge the sky.

When Tate's peculiarly dressed browncoats were ready, a contingent of sun-darkened sailors carrying chests and barrels of powder began to haul them up the beach until Yates managed to commandeer an old cart used to collect driftwood and other debris. A group of fishermen watched the spectacle. Yates waved cheerfully at them. One of them had heard Tate speak and spat to show his contempt.

'Forgive Old Griffin,' Yates exclaimed. 'His brother Gethin was killed by American privateers back in '79. *The Black Prince* bombarded the village after we refused to pay their outrageous ransom. People were killed, a couple of homes were destroyed and St Mary's Church was damaged, but we stood firm against the damned Jonathans!' Yates remembered who he was talking to and muttered an embarrassed chuckle.

'You Welsh are a resolute breed,' Tate remarked stridently, unaffected by the derogatory term for American pirates. 'I take my hat off to you and your people, Mansel.' Tate touched his forelock at the fisherman, but the craggy-faced Welshman offered a black scowl and muttered a curse.

More folk watched the soldiers with suspicious eyes. Yates decided to stroll ahead with Tate as the redcoats and browncoats trailed behind. The climbing path from the harbour was edged with thick tussocks of grass and shouldered with wind-shredded gorse. Cobwebs made silver by damp weather sparkled in the clumps of purple heather. Tate let his eyes wander across the glittering bay,

12

where colonies of razorbills and guillemots nested in the sea cliffs. Many villagers still watched them; the beach was thick with fishermen, nets, boats and fish traps. A salty breeze rushed up the cliff-face, almost knocking Le Haillan's hat from his head. The captain repositioned it and held on to it firmly.

'There's a kittiwake that visits us,' Yates said after a few minutes of silence. 'Aye, he comes down from the embrasures, and Corporal Pritchard feeds it scraps. Aye, that what he calls the bird, Scraps.'

Tate smiled at Yates's enthusiasm for small talk and looked up to the fort. It was a dark shape against the horizon, half-hidden by the rocky ledges, its rampart's top edged with a flickering line of orange to show that braziers burned in the courtyard.

Yates saw his gaze. 'It was constructed back in '81 after the attack. It certainly keeps the bay clear of enemies.'

'Has there been another attack?'

'No,' Yates admitted, 'but it keeps us safe. Just the thought of the guns deterring potential threats gives us a great deal of assurance.'

'How many guns does it have?'

'Eight nine-pounders. Manned by a contingent of Woolwich gunners stationed here.'

Tate did not know where Woolwich was, presuming that it was a place nearby, and so said nothing. The two men exchanged news of past friends, births, marriages and deaths.

Vickers touched the spurs to his horse's flanks to get closer to the two men. He had tried to converse with Marrock, but the morose Irishman promised poor conversation. There was something about Le Haillan that troubled Vickers. He couldn't put his finger on it, so he ignored the too well-dressed Englishman. Maybe that was what bothered him. Days or weeks at sea, and the captain appeared without a stitch out of place. That was odd in Vickers's books.

The ground levelled and the path became flanked with tall grassy embankments. The men's boots echoed loudly in the narrow space.

'And is it true that our old friend William Knox resides in the county?' Tate asked.

'Yes,' Yates replied. 'He has estates over in Slebech and Llanstinan. His son commands two companies here and the two over at Newport.'

'He's done well for himself,' Tate said of the father, and Vickers noted a slight sourness with that comment.

Yates must have noticed the tartness too, for he gave his customary chuckle. 'He has, Bill.'

'What's his son like?'

'Lieutenant-Colonel Thomas Knox is . . . he is a . . .' Yates struggled to find adequate words. He sighed. 'He is a young man,' he said despairingly, hoping that answered it all.

'I look forward to meeting him,' Tate said patiently.

'Indeed,' Yates said rather nervously, which Vickers also noticed. 'Would you like tea, Bill?'

'I would, thank you. I find that I can't function without a cup,' Tate declared.

You Americans wouldn't have any if it weren't for us, Vickers thought mischievously.

The soldiers marched into the stronghold as redcoats watched them from behind the moss-and salt-stained walls. Tate allowed his men twenty minutes' rest. Tea was brewed, provisions were eaten and pipes were lit, but the assiduous colonel took half his men east towards Newport, where dawn blushed the sky a pale pink. Le Haillan and Marrock went northwest, where the land was the highest, up and along the coastal trail past Goodwick, which was a hamlet of fishermen's cottages, and where giant rocky prominences dominated the fields and farmsteads.

Yates went with Tate.

*

A single horseman cantered along the road, which was, in truth, more of a farm track, as the wolf-light of dawn slowly bruised with colour. He slowed the beast down to a trot and then halted it with a steady pull of the reins. The horse obeyed and snorted, its flanks shimmering with sweat in the hazy light. The rider patted its muscled neck fondly and swung out of the saddle. Glancing over his shoulder, he tied the reins to a solitary winter-bare oak tree. A single branch lay on the ground, snapped off from recent fierce winds. He threaded his way down through lichen-haunted stones and grassland interspersed with rock samphire, English stonecrop and wild thyme. The sword hanging from his left hip clanked and rattled. His boots slid on wet grass, but he kept his balance. The waves crashed white against the headland's protruding necklace of rocks, but turning east, they caressed the shore, leaving gentle kisses before rushing back from the arched caves and stony coves.

It was then, above wild tangles of gorse and thinning palls of fog, that he saw masts like inky scratches against the skyline. He edged closer; the smell of the sea filled his nostrils. There were three ships. The first was a large, square-rigged, three-masted frigate; the other two vessels were a corvette and a lugger, each with two masts and fore-and-aft rigged sails. The sails billowed dirty-white against the deep blue-grey of the ocean.

The man produced a telescope from a lard-smeared haversack. He aimed it towards the ships, steadied the long brass tubes with his gloved hands and it took a moment to bring the lenses into focus. His name was Lorn Mullone. He had fought in the American wars and had spent nigh on twenty years watching enemies and deciphering their moves and strategies. And it was his experience and skills that had brought him to this nondescript part of the country, knowing that their appearance here was of no insignificance.

It was quiet except for the sound of the sea and the screeching calls of cormorants and fulmars swooping and diving below.

Mullone studied the ships for some time.

*

John Mortimer, a sixty-year-old sheep farmer, stood on a wildflower rich grassy sward, one of sixteen that he owned, and dropped another pebble into his pocket. His blue eyes drifted across to the grazing sheep and lambs at the northeast of the field, where beyond an oak and alder woodland marked by a stream was Carreg Wastad Point and the tiny cove of Aber Felin. Ravens croaked in the treetops of the wood, where in the spring, the ground would be carpeted with bluebells, foxgloves and crested dog's tails.

'*Deuddeg, tri ar ddeg, pedwar ar ddeg,*' he said, then stopped abruptly because over the soft sigh of the wind and the occasional bleat, he heard the sound of hooves coming from the northeast.

He turned away.

This was nothing out of the ordinary. That road north and the many others joined the main thoroughfares to the villages of Llanwnda, Goodwick and St Nicholas. Many riders used them; farmers and drovers used them. It was surprisingly busy. Mortimer stared at his sheep. '*Pymtheg, un ar bymtheg, dau ar bymtheg, deunaw . . .*'

Something about the frantic sounds of the galloping horse made him turn his gaze again. He strained his eyes at the horseman coming his way, trying to place him, but he couldn't. He saw a glint of red underneath a long grey coat and immediately abandoned counting his flock in groups of twenty.

The horse-soldier saw Mortimer nimbly clamber up onto one of the earth-topped embankments that made the roads in these parts appear to be sunken. He hauled back on the reins, and his grey stallion instantly dropped to a walk.

'Good morning, sir,' he said with a soft Irish accent. He didn't wait for Mortimer to answer him. 'Forgive me for prying, but are you the owner of that farm?' He jerked his head towards the nearest building. Sweat trickled from under his Tarleton helmet and had darkened the edges of his blond hair.

Mortimer studied the stranger. He was a slim built man of about forty. He wore buff-coloured breeches that were patched and worn with age and tall leather boots. A grass-green collar matched his sleeves on the visible scarlet coat, and a scabbard pointed out from the long coat, denoting a sword and thus an officer. The helmet, with its white-over-red plume and black crest, and other accoutrements, including his cream-coloured gloves, were all grimy and weather stained. The Welshman judged that the officer had ridden far.

'Are you the owner of that farm?' the Irishman repeated, this time with more urgency.

Mortimer looked up from the horse's mud-splattered legs and heaving chest and to the man's shadowed green eyes. He had the impression that the officer could soothe the fears of a dozen men

16

with a single look. 'I am John Mortimer, the owner of Trehowel Farm. Who are you?'

'Pleased to make your acquaintance. I am Major Lorn Mullone of Lord Lovell's Dragoons,' the officer said, to which Mortimer gave a little shrug. In truth, Mullone was an officer of a regiment raised in Ireland to fight the risk of invasion, but explaining that right now and what he was doing here was a waste of time, especially since he needed to warn the farmer of impending peril. 'There are three French ships anchored in the bay beyond your land. I would imagine by now they have sent an advance party. Is this the nearest farm? What about other farms?'

'French ships?' Mortimer seemed unable to comprehend such a notion.

'French,' Mullone said sharply, 'and the soldiers will be here shortly, attacking from the landward side. Do you have family with you?'

Mortimer said something in Welsh and then rubbed the back of a hand across his mouth. 'My wife.'

'Get her and any belongings and head south,' Mullone told him, pulling out a folded map with some care from a coat pocket. He examined it. He clenched his jaw which was already pronounced. 'The nearest village is Llanwnda? Is that how it's pronounced?'

'Llanwnda,' Mortimer corrected him, making the 'wn' sound like 'un'. 'It's not far. It's past the heath,' he said, pointing eastwards to where there was a murky smudge in the land. 'There are a dozen homes and St Gwyndaf's Church.'

'What about the local troops in the area?'

A chill wind lifted the woollen scarf about the farmer's neck. 'There's a coastal fort at Fishguard that the Volunteers use,' Mortimer revealed in a tone that said he did not half believe what Mullone had told him. 'Militia or fencibles down at Haverfordwest.'

Volunteers were part-time soldiers who served their own locality while militia were reserve soldiers, and fencibles were full-time, regular soldiers, raised for service within the British Isles.

Mullone grunted. 'That appears to be twelve miles away.'

'More or less. There's a garrison at Pembroke Castle.'

'Even farther,' Mullone said wearily. *Probably a skeletal force that would not be able to match the invaders in numbers or experience*, Mullone thought. 'Are there many farms about here?'

'A handful.'

Mullone looked troubled. 'There isn't time to warn them all. How many Volunteers do they number?'

Mortimer clearly didn't know, but he guessed. 'A hundred. Maybe more. I'm a busy man. I don't have time to count idiots playing at being soldiers,' he said irritably. He rubbed his weathered face and frowned thoughtfully. 'How do you know they're French? Could be our navy on patrol?'

'I know they're French,' Mullone answered firmly, gazing at the headland. 'They've been fighting a strong wind and have moved sluggishly around St David's Head, but they've been looking for a good harbour. I thought they had spotted one about three miles west, but there was a ribcage of blackened wood on that cove, and they carried on.'

'It was a Portuguese ship carrying a cargo of olive oil and wine amongst other things,' Mortimer said. 'The wind brought her onto the rocks. Many a good man have been blown out of this world and into the next. We did well that day,' he added with a sly smile at the spoils of such a wreck.

Mullone half grimaced and put the map away. 'I will ride to Llanwnda and warn them. I know it's asking too much, but can you notify your neighbours to the south of here?'

'I will.'

'Good, and I will also inform the Volunteers of the invasion before it's too late.'

The old farmer blinked. 'Invasion?'

Mullone stared at him. 'What do you think they're here for? The weather? Now get going. Go!'

He made sure Mortimer was indeed making his way home before touching his horse's flanks with his heels and clicking his tongue.

Mullone rode on. He had people to save.

The sky above Llanwnda was a swirling mass of grey cloud, and the sea to the north was a band of silver. High banks of gorse and steep rocky outcrops blocked the views south; fields and meadows stretched away to the east and west. Mullone found it difficult to instil a sense of urgency with the villagers. The priest of St Gwyndaf's Church, Father Bach, a very small man with a birdlike face and fingers as thin as bird bones, objected to the warning.

'God shall smite them!' he shouted with a surprisingly powerful voice. He was wizened and old, and his hoary hair gleamed in the light. A crowd of villagers circled him. '"*You come to me with a sword, a spear and a javelin, but I come to you in the name of the Lord of hosts, the God of the armies of Israel, whom you have taunted"*'! Father Bach thrust a heavy-looking bible up at the sky, his wrists, Mullone saw, were near-skeletal. '"*This day the Lord will deliver you up into my hands, and I will strike you down and remove your head from you. And I will give the dead bodies of the army of the Philistines this day to the birds of the sky and the wild beasts of the earth"*'!'

'That's very inspiring, Father,' Mullone told him, 'but you should take what you can from the church and leave with your flock.'

Father Bach threw him a curious look. His thin arms quivered from holding the Bible still. 'You're Irish!'

'I am, Father.'

Bach nodded with approval, dropping his arms and favouring Mullone with a thin smile. 'You Irish might be a race of beef-heads, but you love three things: God, poetry and violence!'

A smattering of chuckles rose up from the crowd. Sparrows flew from roofs, and a cat, curled up on a barrel, watched the people with sleepy interest.

Mullone's lips curled with amusement. 'I can certainly give you an emotive response now, Father,' he said, then pointed northwards. 'And the approaching French certainly love violence, so I say again,' his perceptive face changed to show exasperation, 'you must leave now! Take what you can and leave no valuables.' He twisted in his saddle, knowing and seeing the fear and befuddlement in their eyes. But this had to be done for the sake of their lives. 'That goes for all of you, leave! Hurry!'

'I will not leave,' Bach rejoined curtly.

'You don't imagine the French are going to leave you and the church silver alone, do you?'

Bach appeared to consider the question for a few moments, almost as though he had never thought about it before. 'No, I don't,' he said mildly, 'but God watches over us, and He will protect us.'

The priest and three villagers stubbornly refused to leave, so they locked themselves in the church. The other folk collected their belongings. One man dressed in black tucked a long-barrelled horse pistol into his belt, and another with the hair the colour of ripe wheat slung an ancient-looking fowling piece over his shoulder and headed to Goodwick. Somewhere a goat bleated noisily. Mullone had dismounted to help a young boy who had dropped a sack containing pewter plates, spoons and other tableware. The boy, who was named Iorwerth, thanked him and Mullone, the last to leave, stepped towards the church and peered through the leper's squint. The oak door had been bolted shut. The silhouette of Father Bach praying below the altar stayed with Mullone as he followed the villagers south.

The road was rutted and still waterlogged from the recent rains. The surrounding countryside reminded him of places of home. Of high heaths and plump meadows, of quick streams and thick woods, of good harbours and stone walls. And there were also larger stone-faced earth banks topped with hedges here, which were difficult to see over, even on horseback. A blackbird swooped across the road between the hedgerows.

'Why are you here?' Iorwerth enquired.

'To warn you of the French.'

'Are you going to protect us?'

'I'm going to do everything in my power to keep you safe,' Mullone said.

'When I need to feel safe, I go up there,' Iorwerth spoke of the gorse-ringed rocky outcrops to the south. 'Those rocks are known as Garnwnda. There's a big stone there like a house. It's got little rooms. Folk say our ancestors built it.'

Mullone wondered if he was talking about the similar ancient stone chambers that dotted Ireland. 'Why do you think they built it?'

The boy shrugged. 'I don't know, but there are bones deep inside. There are a number of the big stones here. My father said giants made them, but I know that's a lie.'

Mullone chuckled. 'You're a bright, boy. When I was a wee boy, I saw a banshee.'

'What's that?'

'It's an Irish fairy that makes a terrible tormented wail and claps her hands. Oh, that howling will freeze your blood. A horrid creature. It is known that men can die of fright if they lay eyes upon her.'

Iorwerth looked genuinely intrigued and frightened at the same time. He then frowned. 'How come you're still alive if you saw her?'

Mullone grinned at him. 'I said you were a bright boy.' He plucked a shilling from his waistcoat, and tossed it to the boy. 'How do you know that giants didn't build the stone houses? Maybe your da is telling the truth?'

Iorwerth shook his head. 'If giants built them to live in, why are they so small?'

'That's a good point.'

'And I found a knife,' said the boy. 'It's made of flint, and it would never fit a giant's hand.'

'That old knife might be worth something one day,' Mullone said.

Iorwerth's lips curled, and he patted his coat pocket.

Mullone heard a bird's cry in the wind and looked up to see a sparrow-hawk hover gracefully over a field. He watched it for a while, then something caught his eye. A speck of light through the winter-dark hedges in the bend south of the road ahead. He wondered what it was. Then more flashes, and Mullone instantly knew it was sunlight reflecting on bayonet tips.

It had to be the local Volunteers or militia, and Mullone was glad to know support was coming, or were most likely on manoeuvres. He clicked his horse to go forward. He was called *Tintreach*, Irish Gaelic for Lightning, because jagged white lines shot up from his hocks. The stallion was a sturdy horse, tall, steadfast and war-trained to kick and bite. *Tintreach*'s ears pricked and he went into a trot. The hooves thudded and the horse furniture jangled, and the militia must have heard Mullone approach, for a command went up and the men

21

halted in the banked road. They were a hundred and fifty yards away.

Mullone's delighted expression dropped like a lead weight down a well. He hauled on the rein and *Tintreach* whickered as though he understood his master's sudden change of glee. The soldiers resembled British troops but were dressed in brown coats, and that instantly drew alarm. Mullone watched an officer, who was staring back, take a few steps forward.

Mullone's eyes widened.

He cursed, knowing who the clever and calculating man was. He unclipped his pistol from his belt and levelled it.

Voices shouted alarm, and suddenly the air was splintered by the pistol's explosion. Birds fled from the hedges and trees.

Mullone turned back to the villagers, knowing the shot would not have hit anyone at that range. 'Get back!' he screamed, the space in front of him swirled with evil-smelling smoke. 'Back!'

Women screamed, men gasped and the folk panicked. A dog barked, and Mullone kicked *Tintreach* back as a small volley tore the air where he had been, but the leaden balls clipped the weed-strewn walls or ricocheted against the ground harmlessly.

A villager, the one with the pistol, was shouting at Mullone.

'I don't speak Welsh!' Mullone bellowed.

'Jesus,' the man said. 'What are you doing firing on people?'

The villager with the fowling piece levelled it towards Mullone. 'You fired on the militia!'

'Put that away, you idiot!' Mullone snarled at him. 'They aren't British militia. They're part of the French invasion force!'

'The what?'

Mullone gave a fleeting look over his shoulder. 'There isn't time to debate this! Get your people back to the crossroads and go south!' He turned to a group who were dithering. 'Go! Go!'

'What will you do?'

Mullone bit his lower lip. 'I don't know,' he said grimly. 'Try to slow them down.'

The black-dressed one thought about that, then tossed the pistol up to Mullone, who caught it clumsily. 'She's loaded,' he said before sprinting away.

22

The yellow-haired man with the fowling piece growled at his departure but hefted the long firearm away from Mullone's form. 'I'll stay with you,' he said in a deep baritone voice.

'You should go,' Mullone told him.

'No foreign bugger is going to tell me what to do, and no foreign bugger invades my land,' the Welshman said and gave a crooked smile to show that he was teasing.

The two of them went back along the road towards Llanwnda, but at the crossroads, the villagers turned south. At the junction, Mullone vaulted from the saddle and reloaded his pistol. The man with the musket was called Hawkins, and he guarded the road. They could hear a scuff of a boot, but Mullone regarded the enemy were wary in case they faced superior numbers in an unknown land.

'Cocksure bastards,' Mullone commented, 'to march like that in broad daylight. Does Goodwick have a good harbour? Is there a good landing spot here?'

'There's no French ships at anchor, only a British one,' Hawkins replied.

Mullone looked at him. 'British?'

'I had to visit my uncle Probert in Goodwick this morning, and that's when he told me about it. It was there this morning. He's a fisherman and was at the harbour when they rowed ashore. Six boats he said. The local Volunteers met them, and off they went to the fort.'

'They aren't British, they are French.'

'How do you know that?'

'Their uniform, although odd, is still British in design, and that may have fooled the Volunteers, but not me.'

'How?' Hawkins asked.

'I recognised one of them,' Mullone said. 'His name is De Marin, and he's a French spy.'

Hawkins's eyes were like boiled eggs. 'A spy?'

Mullone grunted. 'He helped Fouché get rid of Robespierre and works for the Directory. I've known about him for a number of years since Flanders. De Marin is a slippery fellow. Charming, dextrous, fanatical and utterly deadly. My sergeant would say that he could charm salmon from the rivers. Very scholarly, yet equally not afraid to get his hands dirty where it's needed. And the Directory has its hands in a lot of places.'

'He sounds a nasty bugger to tangle with. De Marin,' Hawkins said carefully, as if he was trying to translate it.

'Marine, or seaman, or of the sea,' Mullone returned. 'It could be that he originated from a coastal settlement. I suspect it's just a code name rather than his actual name.'

'Just because he's here doesn't mean the rest of the soldiers are French,' Hawkins pointed out.

'True,' Mullone admitted, 'but I know they are. For the past three weeks I've been trailing the ships. They flew Russian colours and didn't know that they were being watched. They swapped to British colours in the Bristol Channel, but the weather turned sour, and instead of returning to France, they sailed here.'

'Jesus,' Hawkins gaped, 'just who are you?'

'I'm employed by the British government to spy on enemy agents who are trying to bring unrest to British shores. Men like De Marin. Plotting and watching from the shadows like spiders, weaving their webs in the hope of catching their prey. And De Marin, as I said, is a dangerous man, a king of his game, and now he's stepped into the light.'

Hawkins scratched his crotch. 'So you are some sort of spy catcher.'

Mullone peered up at the road. The French may have backtracked or were seeking another route. They were coming, and Mullone had to remain watchful. 'I have yet to catch the man I truly want'. *The spider-king*, he ruminated deeply, *is a truly formidable foe.*

'You will,' Hawkins reassured in his deep voice. 'Why have they come to Wales?'

'Bantry Bay,' Mullone muttered, then he saw Hawkins's puzzled expression. Mullone explained to him that he had intercepted a despatch from an Irish Republican called Wolfe Tone to De Marin. Codes had revealed that thousands of men waited in flat-bottomed barges and troop ships for an incursion. Mullone had subsequently alerted the government to the French armada, and the army managed to repel the landing at Bantry Bay, a small village on the south coast of Cork, two months ago. 'I knew of a second fleet that planned to land in the southwest of the country, perhaps near Plymouth or Bristol. They may well have had other plans to march inland and spread the ideals of liberty to the workers. Anything to cause fear. And they came here to do the same, perhaps thinking that they could unite a bond and start a civil war.'

Hawkins cringed, then shook his head. 'Jesus, more fool us. And now the bloody buggering French are here at my door. I can't believe it.'

'Believe it,' Mullone said with vehemence. 'I haven't heard any sounds of musketry, which tells me no one else suspects their wee *ruse de guerre*.'

Hawkins frowned.

'Their treachery and falsehood,' Mullone explained.

They've now taken the fortress, he said to himself, *without even firing a shot*. They have stores, ammunition, guns and the high ground that dominates the bay and the harbour entrance. Fishguard and Goodwick may now be infiltrated by them. One ship here and the three to the north did not stipulate a massive force. Perhaps fifteen hundred men at the most. But still, it had caught the locals off guard. This was a serious threat.

'How many men did your uncle say there were?' Mullone asked.

Hawkins thought for a moment. 'I think he said about two hundred.'

Two hundred men, probably the elite chosen to garrison the stronghold and secure it. There were not two hundred here now, perhaps a hundred. So Mullone guessed the rest were at the fort. And it meant more than a thousand were to the north.

'There!' Hawkins warned.

The first French appeared a hundred and twenty yards away. They saw Mullone and Hawkins and came slowly, five abreast and at port arms.

'Wait!' Mullone hissed at Hawkins, who was about to pull the trigger. Mullone couldn't see De Marin in the ranks. 'Wait,' he ordered again, hefting the heavy horse pistol in both hands like it was a carbine. He saw *Tintreach*'s long ears twitch and then saw a black form above the stone-faced bank out of the corner of his eye.

He swept the pistol up as a Frenchman appeared, and the ball obliterated the man's face, momentarily leaving a red haze in the air.

'Look out!' Hawkins brought the gun above Mullone, and the shot reverberated loudly. Another Frenchman was plucked violently backwards to meet his maker. 'Sneaky buggers,' Hawkins said as he began to reload.

Three men jumped from the opposite bank, their horsehair manes flapping wildly behind them. The nearest to Mullone, a young officer with hatred in his eyes, stumbled, and Mullone kicked him hard in the throat. The officer was knocked onto his back from the impact, his sword skidding across the ground with a clang. Mullone threw down the horse pistol, the blackened muzzle still smoking, and tugged free his sword. A Frenchman lunged with his bayonet-tipped musket. Mullone battered it aside, slammed his sword forward, felt the blade glance off a rib, twisted it in flesh and then ripped it free. The man grunted and pitched forward. Mullone stepped aside, and a musket exploded close to his face, so close that he felt the passage of wind and the scraps of burnt wadding singe his cheek. He staggered, momentarily deafened, but recovered. Half-blinded by the smoke, he rammed his sword into the powder bank, where to his satisfaction, the blade struck and a man shrieked. Mullone heard grunting and turned around. A Frenchman wearing the white shoulder knot of an NCO was brawling with Hawkins. Both men were gripping the fowling gun, trying to pull it free of their assailant. Hawkins was the taller of the two, but the enemy was stronger, and he was forcing the Welshman back and down to his knees. Just when it appeared Hawkins was losing, he pushed the Frenchman back, kicked his shins, then kneed him in the groin. Hawkins snatched the weapon, reversed it and thumped the heavy stock into the man's face, turning it into a mask of blood.

Mullone looked back at the road, where beyond the haze, the enemy were less than sixty yards away. Hawkins took aim, but a musket boomed from across the opposite bank to send the ball slashing across his forehead. Hawkins collapsed onto his knees, dropping the long-barrelled gun.

Mullone quickly snatched it up, turning the musket on a stocky Frenchman who had just crashed onto the road where the officer was clutching at his gullet, coughing and spluttering, and there were three others dead or dying. The Frenchman snarled as he charged, and Mullone hoped the gun was loaded. He pulled the trigger and was amazed at the savage recoil. The ball punched the enemy as though he had been swatted by an invisible deity, for the force sent him backwards to smash into the stone wall.

Mullone slung the firearm over his shoulders and took a semi-unconscious Hawkins over to *Tintreach*. Blood was pouring down his hair, past his eyes and cheeks, but it was a flesh wound, and head wounds always bled more. He mumbled something incoherent.

Mullone considered their predicament. They could not hope to slow the French anymore, and they were closing fast. He thrust Hawkins's left boot into the stirrup and pushed him up into the saddle, arm muscles screaming with the effort. There was no other option.

'What . . . what are you . . . doing?' Hawkins said groggily.

'You're going south.' Mullone took the Welshman's bag containing loose shot and powder. 'I'm going to draw them away.' He thrust the reins into Hawkins's blood-soaked hands and clasped them tightly. 'Find safety.'

'I can stay!'

'No.'

'You can't go north−' Hawkins was still talking when Mullone slapped *Tintreach*'s rump, and the stallion galloped away.

As quick as lightning, Mullone quipped as he watched them leave. He had not wanted to let them go, most importantly his prized stallion, but he knew he had to. *Keep safe, Tintrí.* The word meant fiery-tempered, for the stallion could prove to be irascible and obdurate. But Mullone would not have him any other way.

He heard boots and voices getting closer, and there was only one thing left to do.

*

Lieutenant-Colonel William Tate was happy. He stared at his pocket watch. It was nearly midday.

'Time for a drink,' he said to the two senior officers crowded in the top floor of the barracks. They were in the officers' quarters and map room; the lower floor was for all other ranks. He poured a generous measure of brandy into three glasses. 'Firstly, I'd like to offer a toast to old friends,' he said, handing Yates and Vickers a glass each. 'Old wood to burn, old stories to tell, old wine to drink and old friends to trust.'

'To old friends,' the three said in unison.

Vickers smacked his lips noisily at the taste, his head inclined as he stared at the deep amber liquid, taking in the heady aroma of spices, fruit, cream and burnt wine. He took another sip and let the fierceness seep down into his cold bones, wondering if the colonel would offer another glass.

There was a timid knock on the door, and Yates seemed to be the only one who had heard it. 'Enter,' he said.

Lieutenant Samuel Nash opened the thick, riveted door and stepped meekly into the room. He was eighteen, with an absurdly young face that was now blushing from the attention. 'Sir,' he saluted. 'Corporal Pritchard has taken his section down to collect the fish, sir.'

'Thank you, Lieutenant,' Yates said.

'Fish?' Tate enquired.

'We are allowed to purchase fresh fish with a little of the money the paymaster allows,' Yates explained. 'Sea trout, whiting, salmon, bass, mackerel and eel. Also chicken, beef and lamb too. Although I'm quite partial to mutton, so I buy that for myself. I like to eat here with my officers, and I can't afford to make an enemy of our paymaster,' he said, winking at Nash.

'We're thinking of expanding the plots so we can grow our own vegetables,' Vickers said. 'We haven't had much success, to be honest. I sowed seeds for barley last year, but blight got to it. I managed to purchase a copy of *The Farmer's Almanac* and hope, with sufficient study, to increase our success this year.'

'Hear, hear,' Yates said.

Tate stifled a yawn. 'Care for some brandy, Lieutenant?'

Nash did not drink, and his mouth twitched as it normally did whenever he was faced with something that was new to him or that he abhorred. He felt too many eyes on him to decline. 'T-Thank you, sir,' he stammered, trying not to show his disapproval, for Nash had been brought up by a strict father who preached against the vices of mankind.

'Good boy,' Yates said. 'Your father disapproves of everything, but there's nothing wrong with brandy. Real men and soldiers drink it. So drink up, that's an order!' His blue eyes twinkled at the naïve young man to show that he was not being serious.

Nash took a tentative sip and then had to suppress the urge to cough and clutch his throat from the harshness of the spirit.

'What employment do you hold when you aren't being an officer?' Tate asked him.

'I work in the counting house, sir,' Nash chirped, eyes watering from the heady drink.

'Samuel, as our paymaster, makes sure the regiment's books are in order,' Yates explained. 'When I tell him to form column, he always checks his accounting books first!' He laughed loudly at his own joke. 'Manoeuvre this, manoeuvre that, young Samuel is a veritable master of figures.'

Nash, uncertain whether he was being mocked, merely smiled.

'Form line,' Vickers said with a guffaw, to which no one laughed.

'What did you think of our manoeuvres this morning, Mansel?' Tate enquired, reaching for a wooden box containing long cigars. The American had brought his men back from the windy moor and down through Fishguard, where the browncoats and redcoats had practised drills and fired three volleys that shattered the morning air with noise. It brought many spectators, and the soldiers marched back to the fort to ripples of applause and children running after them.

'Your men certainly formed from a column and into companies like the drill book, Bill,' Yates said. 'It was a pleasure to watch.'

'Thank you, Mansel,' Tate said heartily, as he offered cigars. Nash hesitated but took one any way. 'Cuban cigars are a luxury many can't afford, but I have a friend who grows Cuban tobacco seeds in Connecticut, and he supplied me with enough cigars for the voyage.'

'How kind,' Yates said.

'I saw you inspecting our guns earlier, sir,' Vickers said to Tate in a tone suggesting he was expecting an answer.

'Yes, Captain,' Tate said, staring at the Welshman with shrewd eyes. 'I'm an infantryman, but I confess an interest in the ordnance. I'm fascinated by it. There's a skill in gunnery. An art, you might say.'

Vickers's face screwed up. 'Art?'

'Yes, art. You can learn to pivot or to shoot disciplined volleys from a book, but with artillery, you have to have a gift. A good eye too. Not everyone has it and that's why a commander of artillery is an artist, so to speak.'

'I see, sir,' Vickers said, though abstractly, as if he merely essayed a courtesy rather than a thoughtful response.

'Your gunners certainly know their business.' The American turned to Yates. 'Veterans from the war with the rebels. I thank you, Mansel, for allowing me to indulge.'

Yates gave a small bow. 'My pleasure, Bill.'

'Seeing the artillery at Brandywine and at the Battle of Guilford Court House, I've become entranced by their design and destructive power.'

Vickers had never seen battle, but he always imagined how he would respond to the clamour of musketry and cannon fire, and the cries of the wounded and dying. Tate, he was certain, was trying to show off his experiences, and that irked Vickers.

'If an attack occurs here,' Vickers voiced boorishly, his sharp eyebrows split his brow like an angry smudge of ink, 'then we don't need the employment of artists. We want the best men for the job.'

'I would assume,' Tate said, 'that you would want that, attack or not.'

Vickers scowled and peered out at the distant hills, where there seemed to be a flicker of light. The sky was heavy with swollen clouds. *Lightning*, he said to himself. It was small but it must be lightning.

Soon the cigars were lit with a tinderbox, the room filled with fragrant blue smoke and the men sat in silent contentment. Nash tried not to be sick. About an hour later, when Yates and Tate were laughing about some old memory, Vickers excused himself to visit the latrine. Nash found the courage to explain that he also needed to go.

'You don't look well, Sam,' Vickers told him as they headed downstairs to the courtyard.

'No, sir.' Nash was grasping his belly.

Upon entering outside, the lieutenant couldn't hold the sourness back and bolted in the narrow space between the armoury and the storehouse to vomit.

Vickers walked away laughing, and when he had finished pissing into the covered pit, a red figure was waiting for him. It was Sergeant Rosser.

'What do you want, Sergeant?' Vickers growled. He was eager to get back upstairs, where there would be more of Tate's brandy and cigars. He felt no qualms for accepting them from a man he was learning to dislike.

'I wanted to speak to you in private, sir,' Rosser said respectfully.

'Here?' Vickers cringed at being too close to the latrines.

'No, sir.'

They moved past the storehouse and stables. Rosser found a secluded spot under the eastern ramparts where they were obscured from the barracks. The sergeant's section of twelve men patrolled the parapets.

'What is it?' Vickers said impatiently. He felt a drop of rain on his cheek.

Rosser sneaked a look over his broad shoulders and then up at the heavens as though he feared God was listening. 'It's about the browncoats, sir.'

'What about them?'

'There's something strange, sir.'

Vickers sighed wearily. 'Strange? In what way?'

'They're an English regiment—militia, and certainly not regular,' Rosser said quietly.

'There are stranger things, Sergeant,' Vickers admonished with a grimace.

'I heard Major Yates mention that they were the 2nd. But 2nd what? 2nd battalion? If so, where are the rest of them?' The sergeant shook his head. 'They speak English, but have you noticed that it's only the officers and NCOs? The other ranks talk, but when you near them, they stop or whisper.'

'I hadn't noticed that,' Vickers confessed, rubbing his chin. The sky was darkening, and the rain was falling harder now.

'Are they a foreign regiment?'

'The colonel mentioned a legion earlier,' Vickers said, 'so perhaps they are from one of those foreign regiments the British Army likes to see on their books nowadays.'

'If that is correct, sir, then where are the rest of them?'

Vickers's black eyes darted up at the barracks, lamplight now giving the windows a bright glow. The truth was that he found Tate and his men with their mud-brown coats odd too, but he was not going to admit that to Rosser in case his intuition was groundless. He found Le Haillan's and Marrock's presence bothersome, but he knew that was no reason for his inner feelings. However, now that the sergeant had brought his concern to bear, Vickers was encouraged to pose the questions to the American in front of Yates. And the sickly, amiable major might just well learn a thing or two.

Vickers was privately furious with Yates's soft command style. He was incapable of maintaining discipline, letting such things fall to Vickers and Rosser all the time. It was a shame that Knox was absent too often, but it was something Vickers was keen to expose, and so tonight he would write the colonel a letter. Did Knox know that Tate and his men were even here? Vickers blinked. Did anyone know? What had Yates said? That they were expected. Is that why the major had disappeared earlier with Tate to talk in private? But what, other than being two old friends, could they be talking about? How the war was won against Mister Washington's men? Vickers growled in anger, more so at himself for not questioning his superiors more. He now looked forward to spoiling Yates's jocular mood and Tate's bluster.

'I will oblige Major Yates and Colonel Tate to answer those pertinent questions, Sergeant,' Vickers said sternly, striding back to the barracks. 'I hope it will put your mind at ease.'

'That it will, sir and thank you.' Rosser snapped to attention, saluted and scuttled away to his men, who watched from the parapets.

Vickers headed to the barracks, heard Nash groan from the shadows, was about to offer some support, but thought better of it. He climbed the stone steps to the officers' quarters, and as he approached the door, he heard the muffled voices of Tate and Yates. Instinct called to him.

He did not open the door; he put an ear to it.

Tate's voice was the loudest. 'We will be seen as liberators, not invaders.'

'You must promise that no villagers will suffer, Bill,' Vickers heard Yates say.

'My mission does not directly involve them, as well you know. As long as they remain unaware, then my men may march south. And you need to hold this fort, Mansel. If I leave a hundred men - my grenadiers - a thousand men could not take it. But I don't know the value of your men. Can they be trusted?'

Vickers, unable to help himself, burst into the room. 'Trusted for what?'

There was a silence, not an awkward quiet, but a realisation that something had now become ruined.

'Trusted for what?' Vickers repeated slowly and angrily.

'Captain . . .' Yates started but seemed bashful. He took a gulp of brandy.

Tate watched Vickers coolly.

Vickers's gaze swivelled to his major. 'Are you in league with the Yankees?'

Yates swallowed hard. 'No, not exactly.'

'What the devil is going on here?' Vickers roared. 'Inform me, and then I shall order Sergeant Rosser to confine you and this . . . colonel,' he said the word as though it had soured his tongue, 'in the damned gaol.' The gaol was the old timber shed.

'I think you've had too much brandy, Captain,' Tate said with levity. 'You're hearing things. We were discussing the last campaign.'

Vickers slammed a hand down hard onto the table, anger rearing again. 'You, sir,' he said , baring his teeth like an animal, 'keep your filthy rebel tongue still.'

'Captain—' Tate started, but Vickers interrupted him.

'Quiet, you contemptible drate-poke!' Vickers returned with the same wolfish bite. He rushed up to Tate, hands balled into fists.

'Dewi—' Yates started.

'I will ask you again about your allegiance,' Vickers said, eyes not leaving Tate. 'Are you in league with the Americans?'

Yates sighed. 'Again, Dewi,' he said, 'not exactly.'

There was a brief pause before the smooth silken sword blade exited through Vickers's chest, grating his breastbone. He looked down at the protruding point as the blood seeped down his coat. Vickers began to shake uncontrollably and tried to speak, but thick, salty blood filled his mouth.

Yates threw his damaged arm around the captain's shoulder and grunted as he clumsily withdrew the blade with his good arm. The action made a terrible sucking sound, and more blood spilled onto the stone floor. Vickers collapsed in a heap.

Tate looked up from the dying man. 'This changes nothing,' he said with grim determination.

*

Mullone could hear French voices above, but none were close. It was dark and cold and damp, but Mullone was concealed, and no man challenged him.

He had fled north towards Llanwnda, drawing the enemy to him with musket and pistol fire, and the farther they followed, the more guarded they became. Then Mullone twisted west and clambered up behind the rock-strewn ridge, where he espied their every move from the heights, without the aid of his telescope, careful not to be seen.

De Marin looked to be in charge, and Mullone knew how desirable his capture was to the French agent. Fifty guarded the connecting roads whilst the other fifty scrambled up the gorse-infested summit in two parties to flank Mullone. But the wily Irishman had known they would do that, so he crawled on his belly down through the gorse as the enemy hurried. They came close but did not spot him. Mullone slithered his way down as quietly as he could, his coat and bags snagging branches and rocks, his fingers and hands filthy, until he knew he was past them.

French voices called out. They were saying that they could not see him and that he must have gone farther north. Mullone allowed himself to smile. But then one of them, possibly an NCO, agreed to climb one of the pinnacles, and Mullone knew he could be spotted from there. What had Iorwerth said? That there was a large chamber somewhere nearby. Mullone turned and gazed up. He could see two men staring east, but that was all. Mullone weaved through a tumble of sharp stones. His knee smacked against them, and he flinched. Then a voice shouted, and Mullone's heart raced. Fearing discovery, he stole a look, but it was from the NCO, who had slipped.

Mullone knew there was little time left before the hunt was over. He had to move now. He pulled himself through a tight gully of rocks, and there he saw a jutting grass-covered hump in the hillside to his right. That had to be it, south-facing and surrounded by large stones. He dragged himself painfully over jagged rocks, and taking a chance, rose up and crept to the entrance.

It was dank, and there was an earthy, slurry sort of smell, not overpowering, yet possibly with faint traces of animal dung. The space stretched back quite far, but it would do, and Mullone waited in shadow, his boots thick with clogging mud. He could see Fishguard's peninsula. Smoke from coal and wood fires hazed above the roofs, gulls screeched, but there was no telltale signs that an enemy had landed and were causing mayhem.

Mullone waited for a long time to make sure no enemy were nearby. He had his pistol and sword ready. Hawkins's clumsy musket had been discarded, for in the skirmish the mainspring had gone, rendering it useless. A gunsmith with his tools would be able to remove the lock, the frizzen, various springs, screws and then replace a new mainspring for complete reassembly.

Mullone shivered. He couldn't feel his toes. He skulked awkwardly from the dark recesses to the chamber's entrance, awash with dull overcast light. Mullone brought out his telescope and aimed it down to the harbour where the French frigate lay at anchor. He knew that the ship was either *La Vengeance* or *La Resistance* from his intelligence reports, but he didn't know which. He also knew that the fleet was commanded by Jean-Joseph Castagnier, a middle-aged commodore of some repute. So who commanded the land operations? De Marin? No, Mullone cogitated. The man was an agent, nothing more. For success, the French must use an experienced infantry commander.

There were lights coming from the fortress and redcoats on the ramparts. It was good news, but something niggled. Were the redcoats working with the French or not? He could not see any of the conspicuous browncoats. Hawkins had said there were two hundred. One hundred under De Marin had gone north to meet the others, Mullone was sure of that, so where were the rest? Had Llanwnda's villagers raised the alarm? The only sound had been the wind that had picked up so that the gorse shook. There was also the distinct sound of musketry far to the north or northwest, but any popping over two or three shots had long died. So far, it seemed the French invading army was completely undetected. He checked his timepiece; it was nearly two o' clock.

Mullone's thoughts turned back to the stronghold again and the most important question: was it in British hands? He had to find out. Lives were at stake and it was his job.

Mullone stepped out and made sure there were no enemies present before threading his way down the rippling grass towards Fishguard.

The rain was coming down in shifting curtains, glimmering the cobbled roads and drumming on rooftops. Dull yellow lights streamed from windows. Mullone, with his helmet, tall cavalry boots and pistol and sword half-concealed by his long coat, was a sight that garnered a lot of suspicion by the villagers of Fishguard. Particularly when he had revealed to a group who had asked him who he was and what had happened today. They gaped with incomprehension, thinking him straight from Bedlam.

'The only foreigner I can see is you,' said a tar and salt-encrusted man.

'Man looks like a beggar,' another said, jerking a thumb at Mullone's unkempt and dirty appearance. He turned to one of the other fishermen hauling on tackle at the harbour. 'Here, Alban! Is this what you've been trawling up?'

'He stinks like a whale's fart!'

Mullone let the burst of raucous laughter die as he scanned the fort with his glass from the shadows of the nearby inn. He could see redcoats at the walls, but that meant nothing.

'And which regiment are you from, sir?' a new voice disturbed him, and Mullone turned to see a tall man in his fifties, dressed in plain but neat clothes with a fur-lined cloak and woollen cap. The man took a step forward with the aid of a walking stick of polished ash. He had a clean-shaven face, a large bony nose and a wide wrinkled forehead.

'Lord Lovell's Dragoons, sir. Ireland,' Mullone added and then wondered why he did.

'May I ask what brings you all the way here?' The man smiled as he asked it.

'You may,' Mullone responded irritably because he was tired. 'The French.'

The man raised a quizzical eyebrow and said something Mullone was not expecting.

'In that case, you had better come with me.'

'The oyster pie is very good,' Captain Thomas Nisbett said to Mullone. 'So is the cawl and bara lawr. Nice flitch of bacon will do you well. The Old Ship serves rare food.'

Mullone's eyes surveyed the cosy inn. No one seemed to take any notice of them in the corner of the room, sitting next to one of the harbour-facing windows. A candle stub guttered on the ledge.

'I don't have time to eat,' Mullone said to the officer, who revealed he had retired from the army and was now on half-pay. 'I must tell someone of the treachery.' He knew he sounded pathetic, but he was as famished as he was bone-weary. It must have been four, maybe five days since he'd eaten a hot meal. He had been eating inn-bought dried meat, bread and cheese in the saddle.

'My dear fellow,' Nisbett said, 'you have told someone. Me. And you can allow yourself a few minutes' rest before we act. You look positively done in.'

Mullone looked at him. 'We?'

Nisbett smiled, which turned into a beam that took over his entire face. 'Of course. Now there are two of us that the locals think are mad.'

Mullone allowed a grin. A short woman with long black hair and jowls hanging below her chin brought ale and a bowl filled with hot water for Mullone to wash his hands. Nisbett ordered oyster pie and broth.

'Ale too,' Nisbett told her, then looked at Mullone with an eyebrow raised.

Mullone nodded. 'That'll be sufficient.'

'Good,' Nisbett snorted with approval. 'Thought you might be some damned Methodist that supped Adam's ale,' he said, meaning water.

Mullone paid for the provisions, to which Nisbett looked outraged, but he relented. The woman took out a short clay pipe from her apron and disappeared to cook the food. Two men seated nearby eating a plate full of white crab, lobsters and cockles laughed raucously. One of them had a wooden leg, a legacy of the wars. A boy sat near the hearth that was burning brightly with coals; a great dog lay across his lap, both seeking comfort and warmth.

'It's been many years since I was fighting the king's enemies, but I can smell the powder and blood on you,' Nisbett said, a fiery glee in his eye. 'I assume that's not your blood.'

Mullone dried his hands with the provided cloth. He flexed his fingers, feeling warmth slowly creep back into his marrow. 'No.'

Nisbett chuckled. 'Good God, man, I hope you didn't just tickle him.'

'He won't be laughing again,' Mullone replied and then frowned at the levity. He loosened the white silk neck-tie about his throat. His helmet, bags and pistol were on the floor, and his wet coat hung from a nail in the wall. 'Did you fight in the Colonies?'

Nisbett nodded. 'I was a captain of the Light Company, 5th Foot. You saw service?'

'I did indeed,' Mullone brooded. He knew he sounded vague, but he didn't know the friendly captain yet well enough to indulge in his past activities. He had fought the king's enemies for nigh on twenty years and had been in a dozen battles and skirmishes. 'A lot of time has passed by, but sometimes it feels like only yesterday I was over there.'

'I fought the Yankees for a couple of years, but then the regiment was sent to Saint Lucia, where we switched to killing the damned Crapauds.' Nisbett gave a strange bark of a laugh, then sighed. 'God, I hated that place. The heat, the food and the damned sweating. Glad to go on the books after that. Whereabouts from Ireland do you come from?'

'A little place near Westport, County Mayo.'

'You miss it?'

'Aye, I do.'

Mullone loved to ride through the rich green pastures or along the shoreline of Clew Bay, fish the Carrowbeg River and sketch from the summits of the *Trosc Mór* and *Cruach Phádraig* mountains. Ireland, he thought longingly, as sweet as God intended.

The food arrived, and Mullone ate ravenously. Nisbett enquired after some port and cheese, but Mullone would take no more. He was full and eager to resume with his task.

'So tell me, Major,' Nisbett started to eat his cheese, but it crumbled under his touch, 'what the hell is going on?'

Mullone told him he worked for the government and everything that had happened, and Nisbett was gracious enough to listen to it all. 'So I need to get up to that fort. Find out if the Volunteers are aware of the duplicity and hope to warn the regional commanding officer of the French frigate and the landing at,' Mullone paused as he pulled out a map, 'Carreg Wastad. Do you know who commands locally?'

'That'll be Lieutenant-Colonel John Campbell, Lord Cawdor,' Nisbett said helpfully. 'He has estates here in Pembrokeshire, Cardiganshire and Scotland, I believe. He commands the Castlemartin Yeomanry Troop. They'll all be down at

Haverfordwest and Pembroke. The only armed units are the Volunteers here and over at Newport.'

Mullone went to move. 'Now I know the French are here for definite, I must get word.'

'I'll do that at my lodgings, old chap,' the old veteran said. 'I'll send correspondence to Lord Milford and to the colonel of the Pembrokeshire Militia. He's called Colby, and he's a decent fellow. They'll mobilise soon enough.'

'I had hoped the villagers from Llanwnda and the farmsteads might have reached here by now,' Mullone said with a frown. 'I sent them south. I wonder where they have gone? One of them is wounded.'

'I'm sure they've made it to safety,' Nisbett said, draining his ale pot. 'Probably made their way down to St Nicholas or Granston or Haverfordwest. I also need to inform Sir William Knox, another landowner with contacts, and whose son is the commanding officer of the Fishguard and Newport Volunteers. Sir William made his money from the war with the Americans, and his obnoxious son lives off the tenants' rents. Both men have contacts and enemies.' Nisbett chuckled. 'I will also send word to Captain Longcroft, Royal Navy Regulating Captain for Milford and Haverfordwest. He's a very important person to know in these parts. He'll have ships, artillery and Jack Tars at his disposal. Although the locals won't like me bringing him here,' he said with a smirk.

'Why not?'

'Press gangs, of course. They'll be crawling around here like lice on a whore's crotch. There are a few men who hide in their cottages to escape impressment. Or disappear to the woods and hills. Longcroft will search for men. The navy is damned greedy. Always needing men. But this is war,' he said savagely, 'and I damned well knew something was amiss today.'

'How so?'

'I was taking my morning stroll when I came across the Volunteers and a queer-looking company marching through the village,' Nisbett explained. 'Brown coats instead of red. Good God, man. Soldiers not in red. What's the army coming to? They'll be parading in white or yellow or green next! So I studied them. They marched well, and they seemed steady, fit and well trained. Not British though. Some foreign regiment in pay, I thought. But my old soldier's intuition was screaming out. I watched that ship out there too and thought about those damned browncoats, the French landing in Ireland that's been in all the papers, and I knew something was wrong. These are dismal times, but we must be prepared.'

Mullone tried to fight off a yawn and lost. His body was screaming out for sleep. He pushed back his chair and reached for his coat. 'My sentiments exactly.'

'But it was this that confirmed my theories.' Nisbett brought out a folded piece of paper and moved it across the table to Mullone. 'Here, read this.'

Mullone unfolded it carefully. It was a pamphlet called *The Compatriot*, and it spoke to the people of Wales to follow in the pursuit of freedom by throwing off the yoke of English slavery. It said that the Welsh should be governed by their own people, not by a corrupt English Parliament, have its own laws and follow the freedom achieved by the people of France, where there was good order and good government. Liberty, equality and fraternity for all of Wales.

Mullone looked up to Nisbett. 'Where did you get this?'

'Oh, they were secretly dropped at the harbour this morning. A whole damned stack of them.'

'I was wrong about the French,' Mullone said, peering at the words again. He moved a thumb over the ink, which smeared, denoting it was printed recently. 'I thought their plan might be to land at Bristol and then move north to Liverpool and Manchester. Places where there have been unrest and riots. It's the sort of thing they like to do: fan the flames of strife. This tells me they planned to come here anyway.'

Nisbett scoffed. 'No matter. The Welsh aren't fools. That goes for the damned Methodists too. I was going to wipe my backside with that seditious nonsense.'

'May I keep it?'

'Of course,' the captain snorted.

Mullone tucked it away in a pocket. 'Now if you can send word, I'll go spy on the garrison.'

Nisbett made a face. 'You're not thinking of just marching up to the gates, are you?'

Mullone shook his head. 'I don't know what to expect, so I'll find another way in, if I can. It'll be dark soon, and that's good because I'll need stealth.'

'Going there is ringing a bell you won't be able to unring.'

'True.'

'You need sleep, man.' Nisbett thumped the table.

'It will have to wait.'

'What will you do when you get there?'

Mullone rose, put his coat on and shrugged. 'I guess I'll find out when I'm there.'

Nisbett appeared to be thinking. 'Wait.' He rammed his hat on his head. 'There's someone I know of who can get you up there, and most likely inside.'

Mullone turned to him. 'Oh?'

The captain went over to the boy with the dog and spoke to him. Mullone couldn't hear what was said, but the boy took a fleeting look at him before darting outside. A moment or two passed and the boy returned and bobbed his head at Nisbett.

The captain gestured that Mullone follow, and soon the two of them were outside, where daylight was fading. The western sky pulsed a deep red, and its light was reflected in lurid, shifting ripples across the bay, throwing their shadows far ahead. Luckily, the rain had stopped. Rats scurried away from the men. The veteran walked surprisingly well for someone with a stick. 'Short walk up here,' he said.

A figure stood at the top of the road. Mullone was surprised to see it was a youth waiting beside a stone wall leading to a cottage. The home was brushed by the sun's scarlet fire.

Nisbett reached the boy first and spoke in a low voice. Mullone saw him nod after the exchange. 'This is young Arthur Cadoc,' Nisbett said. 'He's agreed to take you to the fort.'

'Agreed?' Mullone asked.

Nisbett smiled. 'For a guinea, of course.'

Mullone's mouth creased to a hard line. 'What about doing this for the love of your country?' he asked the boy.

'I am,' Cadoc grinned. 'That guinea will be well spent on ammunition.'

'Arthur has ideas of becoming a Volunteer, or even hug Brown Bess with the regulars,' Nisbett said proudly. The two of them had formed a strong bond over the past two years. Nisbett would regale the boy with his stories of America and read to him of the Sugar Islands, India and China in exchange for fresh seafood. 'I have also let him use my old musket I brought back from the wars. I must admit, for a sixteen-year-old, he's a better shot than me and most of the men from my old company. And some of them were fine marksmen.'

'Thank you, Captain Nisbett,' Cadoc said, his smoke-coloured eyes glinting in the light. He was of average height, lithe, and his coal-black hair poked out from a grey woollen cap. 'I hope I can shoot the bastards tonight,' he said, and for the first time Mullone saw a pack and the short barrel of a carbine slung over his shoulder.

'What are you doing with that?' Mullone demanded, wondering if it was in fact Nisbett's.

The boy bridled. 'It's mine, Major. I bought it.'

'From who?'

'The Volunteers.' Cadoc jerked his head towards the fortress. 'One from their stock of weapons. They wanted twenty shillings for it, but I paid for it with wine.'

'Wine?' Mullone said, astonished.

'Portuguese wine, Major. From a wreck on the coast.'

Mullone remembered that the farmer, John Mortimer, had mentioned the shipwreck. Now government firearms were being bought with wine. He thought to castigate the boy, but it was not his fault there was black market trading. It went on everywhere. 'I don't need you to accompany me inside,' Mullone said instead. 'It's too dangerous. What's your father going to say?'

Cadoc shuffled his feet. 'He won't care either way, Major,' he said with a determined look.

Mullone bit his lower lip. 'Very well,' he said, 'but you obey my commands, do you hear?'

Cadoc gave a mock salute. 'Yes, Major.'

'And your carbine remains unloaded,' Mullone insisted, thinking that the boy had a hunter's watchful face. Nothing would get past him. 'Is that understood?'

Cadoc's shoulders sank slightly. 'Yes, Major,' he said weakly.

'Good.'

The sound of hooves filled the air, and a young man wearing a British infantry officer's uniform appeared on the road leading southwards. His boots and white breeches were spotted with mud.

'It's Colonel Knox, commanding officer of the Volunteers,' Nisbett announced quietly for Mullone's sake.

'You there!' Knox bellowed down at the group. 'Do you mind telling me where I can find an Irish major?' Mullone stepped out from the shadows, and Knox saw the sword at his hip and his crested Tarleton helmet. 'It is Mullone, isn't it?' Knox guessed, but was now met with a stare of incomprehension. 'Well, is it or isn't it, man?' Knox demanded brusquely.

Mullone, recovering from his astonishment, nodded. 'It is, sir.'

Thomas Knox had light-coloured hair that framed a thin face, with cheeks reddened by exertion, perhaps of a long ride, but then Mullone smelled strong alcohol on his breath. 'I've been told by civilians up from Pen Caer that you've spotted a French landing party.'

'Yes, sir.'

'My, my, you have been resourceful,' Knox said, his tone slightly mocking. 'So it was you that sent the villagers south, eh? They came bleating into St Nicholas, where upon I heard the news at Granston. Interrupted a social gathering, but I rode here as quick as I could. After all, one has to do one's duty.'

Mullone frowned at Knox's flippancy. 'Are they all right?'

That seemed to take Knox by surprise. He pursed his lips and stiffened in the saddle. 'They'll be fine,' he replied tartly. 'I have your horse, Major.'

A wave of relief swept over Mullone. *Tintreach was safe. Thank God.*

'My sincerest thanks to you, Colonel.'

'A fine stallion. He must have cost you a pretty penny.'

Mullone's head bobbed. 'Aye, but he is worth it, sir.'

'Ireland breeds good horses.'

'It does, Colonel.'

Knox saw Nisbett and Cadoc for the first time. 'What are you doing now?' he asked Mullone, who then explained his plan. Knox grimaced. 'And then do what exactly?' he asked suspiciously.

'If I can fire a round from one of the guns,' Mullone said, 'then that should alert you as to the security. If I fire it, consider it in our hands.'

Knox glared at him. 'You mean to say my men have turned their coats?' he said hotly.

'I don't know what's happened, Colonel,' Mullone said patiently, 'but at least a hundred Frenchmen wearing British uniforms dyed dark brown have infiltrated the fort.'

That was news to Knox. 'Preposterous!' he blurted.

'It's true, sir.'

'Colonel Knox, I have seen the enemy march with your Volunteers through the village this morning,' Nisbett told him. 'I've seen them practise musket drill together. It does not mean they've turned their coats. They may have been deceived.'

'How many of the enemy are there?'

'Varying reports,' Mullone revealed, 'but perhaps a hundred hereabouts. And there's a Frog frigate anchored in the harbour. A new French ship of the line, heavily manned and with forty-eight guns. Armed with heavy eighteen-pounders, a broadside could destroy the garrison in an instant.'

Knox wiped his mouth that had hung slack. 'I know what a frigate is, man!' He glowered towards the bay, but houses and a large storehouse blocked his view of the ship. 'I have already sent word to the garrisons at Pembroke and Haverfordwest for assistance. I have ordered the Newport Volunteers to march here with all haste,' he said as though that countered what was stacked against them. 'With Major Yates's command, we'll have two hundred and seventy armed men by midnight.'

'Major Yates?' Mullone asked.

'Major Mansel Yates, my second,' Knox told him. 'And that's enough men to take back the fort, if it is indeed in enemy hands.'

Mullone winced, and Nisbett blew out a lungful of breath.

'If the French hold it, sir,' Mullone ruminated, 'you'll lose a lot of men trying to retake it. And what of Major Yates's men? They might be prisoners for all we know.'

'It can be done,' Knox answered fervidly.

'Not if the frigate opens fire,' Nisbett warned.

'We must try,' Knox said stubbornly.

Mullone thought the colonel very untutored. Young, brash and aloof, he was the typical officer in command of local forces. Inexperience, Mullone knew, could bring disaster.

'I will go with young Arthur,' Mullone said in the tone that required no objection. 'I think it prudent to watch and guard the roads to Newport, and once you have the men, sir, scout north to find how far the French have got. I would imagine by now that they've made significant headway.' Mullone revealed what he had seen at dawn and the pursuit up to Garnwnda.

Knox blanched and fiddled with the reins. 'How many are we facing in total, Major?'

'Perhaps fifteen hundred, sir.'

'Is that a mere guess?'

'No, sir.' Mullone bit his lip at the impertinence to his intelligence.

The look on the young colonel's face was suddenly a sign of desperation and terror. 'Then we must . . .' he said, then faltered into gloomy silence.

Mullone gave young Cadoc a serious look before the two of them left to follow the track across the bluff, where Mullone had a job to do.

*

Tate glanced at his timepiece, smiled and walked to the window. He peered at the frigate and shone a lamp at the glass. He took it out of sight momentarily, then back again. He did this three times. He watched and waited. A small light shone from the poop deck back at him three times. There was the signal he had been waiting for.

'There,' he said happily, 'it's done. *La Resistance* is rejoining the fleet at Carreg Wastad.'

Yates tore his gaze from the map spread on the table. 'That's good news.'

'Yes, and now we can start our next objective.'

'My men do worry me,' Yates remarked.

Tate lit another cigar. 'Worry you? You think they've guessed?'

The major hesitated, not wanting to introduce a note of pessimism on an evening of success. 'No, but I don't think they are likely to follow our cause. I had suspected I might see a third of them show an interest in marching with us against the English, but now I doubt it.'

'Would they fight against us?' Tate asked. The tip of the cigar briefly burned orange as he sucked the smoke into his mouth.

'No.'

There had been a small spark of Welsh Unitarianism in the last couple of years, but the talk of rioting had always been inaugurated by the economy. Tudor Rees, a weaver from the south, had preached a Welsh version of the Rights of Man and the 'Marseillaise'. He had tried to make the French victories in the Italian mountains an example of what the Welsh could do in their mountain villages, but it had fallen on deaf ears. He had visited Fishguard hoping to convert a few locals only to be pelted with horse manure.

'Do you think your sergeant will come here snooping around?'

Yates considered Sergeant Rosser for a moment. He glanced at the body of Vickers in his cot, hidden underneath his mantle, then down to a blanket covering the bloodstains on the floor. 'No, he wouldn't,' Yates said. 'And I possess the solitary key to the door.'

'Then there is nothing to fear.' Tate smiled. 'Your Volunteers would be about as threatening in battle as muskets primed with kisses.' He laughed loudly at his own joke. 'They play at soldiering. My grenadiers would eat them alive. Even if they battled the local militia, they are worth ten militiamen a piece. Here, they are wolves amongst the sheep.'

Yates recoiled slightly at the scorn against his countrymen. 'I would still wish for more men,' he said quietly. He wondered if Tate had forgotten *Général* Lazare Hoche's strict instruction that they were not to engage with regular forces, but to fall back if threatened.

'I would wish for the same,' Tate said fervently, 'but we must make do with what we've got. The Black Legion will do us proud, Mansel,' he said, using the English name for *La Seconde Légion des Francs*, nicknamed *La Légion Noire* for the dark colour of their coats. 'Don't forget, six hundred of our men are battle experienced. I'd wager they'd defeat a redcoat battalion any day. And as you know, the redcoats, are disciplined. I will admit that they are good, damned good. I admire their training and their steel discipline. They are trained to stand in line and exchange musket volley after musket volley. We both know how quick they can fire. But out there,' Tate peered out of the window, 'they aren't trained to fight in loose order in the rocky hills and the deep woods. The core of the Black Legion have fought in such terrain. We have the edge here, Mansel. We shall strike like vipers and spread the one thing that will shred the damned redcoats like canister shot: fear. That is why we shall win.'

'Amen,' Yates said, thinking inwardly that the remaining eight hundred of the legion were prisoners of war, royalists, deserters and convicts and weren't worth a damn.

'And they have an American leading them! One that fought and beat the redcoats!'

'Amen to that.'

There was a pause as Tate walked over to the table and studied the map. His eyes creased over the spidery ink scratches and lines of Wales. 'With the north part of the cape now secured,' he traced a finger around Carreg Wastad, 'and no resistance met with the landing, so far so good. I'll send one of our best men on your captain's horse to inform Le Brun of our success and instruct him to ride back if the aristocrat has any problems.' Jacques-Phillippe Le Brun was once an officer in the Royal Army of France but had decided to join the revolutionaries. He was a competent officer who had tamed some of the outspoken royalists and sympathisers during the voyage, and, as Tate's second, he was in charge of the shore parties to the north. 'With our efforts still hidden, we will link up and make our way here,' he said, eagerly tapping an area. 'Here is where we go tomorrow.'

Yates didn't need to see what the American was specifying because he knew: Llanstinan Manor, one of the homes belonging to

Sir William Knox, whom Tate had called an 'old friend' on his arrival. This was an untruth because Tate utterly despised him. A hatred borne from when Sir William was the Under-Secretary of State for the Colonies and was instrumental in an act of war that saw Tate's family murdered by pro-British Native Americans. Tate had found out that Knox was involved, but suddenly the war ended, and the British sailed home. Tate had kept up correspondence with Yates, who was a rebel spy, and had returned to Pembrokeshire after being discharged from the army. He wrote that Sir William had purchased estates in the county, and Tate's plan for revenge burned.

And now, using Hoche's initial order to execute a *coup de main* for terror by spreading French propaganda, burning Bristol, demanding a ransom from the city, rescuing prisoners aboard prison hulks and manipulating the workers to start riots, Tate would look for vengeance against the man who had ruined his life.

The American had felt a twinge of worry that the voyage might prove unlucky, but abandoning their primary mission was actually a blessing. Knowing that Sir William Knox was here, just a few miles away, was enough for Tate to thank his good fortune.

Tate stabbed Llanstinan with a finger and then drew it south towards Slebech. 'And there, "revenge should have no bounds",' he said darkly.

*

Mullone was crouched low. The moon coasted across a lacework of clouds, giving little light, so that to the north there was a promontory of low, shadowed ground that jutted into the bleak waters. The frigate had begun to slowly sail away, and Mullone knew it was joining the other ships off Carreg Wastad Point. There was safety in numbers, especially from the prowling Royal Navy. But if the French had to make a tactical withdrawal, then they would seek out the ships, which meant that the fort would be abandoned. Maybe, he thought, the stronghold was not a concern of theirs, merely just a temporary base. Or perhaps there were significant stores of ammunition there, which they were going to steal and then use.

Mullone still had questions when Cadoc signalled with a hand that they should move.

Mullone lurched as he crossed tussocks and rocks to the imposing walls. They had waited for over two hours for the dusk to settle, and his limbs were now stiff from the cold. He held on to his scabbard to stop the straps from jangling, fearing the noise of their boots and their clothes, but no one had seen them or called out in alarm. Cadoc took him around the great circular northwest bastion, where a union flag flapped noisily above it, along to the north eastern one and back towards the mainland. There he stopped.

'What is it?' Mullone murmured.

Cadoc gaped up the walls and, whirled about, searching the knee-high heather and grass for something. Then he grinned and pulled a ladder seemingly from the earth itself just as Mullone was beginning to wonder how he was to get over the walls.

'They won't be expecting me tonight,' Cadoc said, shaking and pulling clinging heather from the ladder.

'Expecting you?'

Cadoc rubbed a finger under his nose. 'Aye. I usually don't make my rounds until the end of the month.'

'Rounds?' Mullone asked, staring, as they steadied the ladder against the thick walls.

'I do a bit of trading with the Volunteers,' Cadoc revealed. 'Tobacco, wine, brandy, fish, crab, lobster, whatever I can get my hands on.'

'And where do you get them from?'

'Wrecks, fishing and other trading, Major.'

Mullone looked up at the ramparts and bastions but could not see if anyone was watching them back. A bat flitted overhead. 'And what do you trade for exactly?'

Cadoc gawked at the Irishman as though he was babbling. 'Money, Major,' he said, exasperated.

The wind whipped cold, and Mullone shivered under his damp greatcoat. 'I thought that you were going to say arms and ammunition,' he said dryly.

The boy grinned. 'Sometimes.' He looped the carbine over both shoulders with the leather strap, then put a boot on the first rung. 'I'll go first. They won't be expecting me, but they know me. I'll call you up when the coast is clear.'

Mullone reached out and gripped Cadoc's arm. 'If you get an inkling that something is wrong, you leave immediately.'

'I will, Major,' Cadoc said, grinned again, then began to ascend speedily like Jack Tars climbing rigging.

Mullone watched the boy; the wood creaked and squealed with each step, but it held firm.

A tense few moments passed by. Stars twinkled in the black sky. The moon's bright reflection glimmered across the sea and sparkled the stonework. Mullone could see a few scattered lights from homesteads to the east but could see nothing stirring in the distant twilight. It had been, to most people, just another day. In the blackness, an owl hooted. Mullone fancied he could hear its wings beating feverishly.

'Major,' a voice whispered from above, almost soundless. It was Cadoc.

Mullone craned to decipher the next move, and then the boy waved an arm, so Mullone began to climb.

*

Sergeant Rosser was in a fitful mood.

Captain Vickers had not been seen since the officers had had their luncheon, and despite every attempt to acquire his location, Major Yates had discounted his enquiries with his usual congenial vagueness.

'Too much brandy,' Yates had revealed, which was not a gracious thing to say about a fellow officer. He realised that and then immediately added further comment. 'The captain is feeling rather unwell, and so I have instructed him to rest in his bed. Rest, rest and more rest. That's the cure.'

Even Lieutenant Nash looked uncharacteristically ill, and a changeover of the sentries at eight o' clock gave Rosser a further concern as the browncoats had been ordered for an hour's manoeuvre on the heath before returning to their billets in the abandoned farm. The American colonel seemed energetic and infused with enthusiasm as he led eighty of his men out of the gates. 'My men can march and fight whatever the time of the day, Sergeant,' he had crowed.

Rosser watched the men march with the ease and swagger of veterans. The sergeant began to sing 'Yankee Doodle', a song sung by the British during the American Revolutionary War, which mocked the colonials as a dishevelled and disorganized rabble.

Yankee Doodle came to town,
for to buy a firelock.
We will tar and feather him,
and so we will John Hancock.

If Tate heard, he ignored the blatant impertinence. Twenty of his men still remained inside the fort, commanded by a large sergeant with a waxed moustache who glared at Rosser with suspicious eyes.

'Bloody cribbage-faced foreigners,' Rosser grumbled under his breath. They looked a lean ugly bunch, with pitted faces like the holes of a cribbage board. He strode away whistling the tune as loudly as he dared. As duty sergeant, he made sure the sentries had mugs of tea and stood in the south eastern bastion where two of the nine-pounders guarded the undulating neck of land. He shared a joke with the men and finished his drink before ambling across the gatehouse to the south-western tower. All was quiet and well, he reasoned. He then walked to the north, where he was accosted by Corporal Pritchard, a mousy-haired man with a round face and large eyes who worked in the port's herring fishery.

'Sergeant, Alban Cadoc's boy is here,' the corporal told him and then said something else that was inaudible.

Rosser frowned, then stole a glance up at the officers' quarters, hoping not to see the major watching. Thankfully, the window was empty. 'What's all this about, boy?' Rosser was cross, not because he disapproved of Cadoc's scheme, but because he didn't have enough money to purchase any tobacco. 'You are early,' he said, then stopped dead, puzzled, because an officer was striding towards him, with Pritchard looking grim in tow. 'Sir?'

'Sergeant Rosser,' said the officer with a commanding yet respectful tone. 'I need a word with you. Now, if you please.'

Rosser noted the man was Irish. 'Sir!'

'My name is Major Mullone, and I have rather sensitive information I need to impart.'

Rosser suddenly looked uncomfortable.

Mullone understood the NCOs thoughts. 'This is nothing about what arrangements you may have with the boy here.' He gestured to Cadoc, and Rosser relaxed a little. 'Sergeant, I understand from Corporal Pritchard that there are browncoats herein.'

'Yes, sir.'

'And Major Yates is in the barracks.'

'He is, sir. Shall I get him?'

'No, not yet,' Mullone said. 'Where are the rest of the Volunteers?'

'Sections chosen for sentry duty tonight are garrisoning the barracks, sir. Along with the gunners; a team of invalids, sir. Royal Artillerymen from Woolwich. The rest of the Volunteers are billeted in the field to the east. Full turn out. The major said that Colonel Knox wanted us to march as an honour guard.'

'Where?'

'I don't know, sir. That information was not shared with me.'

'I see. And where are the rest of the browncoats?'

'Beyond the field there is an old farm, sir. They billet there, but their colonel just took eighty of them out on manoeuvres. The rest are what you can see.'

'Do you know the name of the colonel?'

'It's Tate, sir. And he's a Yankee.'

An American in French pay. Mullone had not heard the name before, but Tate must be proficient, because the French Directory had requested his presence in this incursion.

'Major Yates knew him, sir. They were old friends from the war. Used to write to him every couple of months. The major always spoke highly of him.'

Mullone reflected his next words for a moment. 'What I'm about to tell you may shock you, Sergeant. The browncoats are in fact French troops.'

Rosser gulped. 'Bloody buggering hell!' he rasped, then apologised for his language. 'I knew something wasn't right, sir. I told the captain about my thoughts this afternoon.'

Mullone narrowed his brilliant green eyes. 'And what did he say?'

'He said he would raise my concerns with Major Yates, sir. But I haven't seen him since. When I asked after him, the major told me he was unwell.'

Mullone looked across the courtyard to where the browncoats were gathered around a couple of braziers. None were on watch, yet they were close to the gates, and that to Mullone suggested that Tate had left them to guard it. 'Your major,' he asked the barrel-chested NCO, 'do you trust him?'

Rosser bit his lip, then scowled. 'I'm not sure, sir. Something is going on, and my guts have never let me down.'

Mullone nodded as though satisfied with the answer. 'Then we'll go with your guts, Sergeant, and leave the major out of what we're going to do.'

'Do, sir?'

'We'll start with arming your men in the barracks. I want muskets loaded and bayonets fixed. Leave the sentries as they are, but notify them of who the browncoats really are. I want the rest of the Volunteers brought into the fort. We must not panic, or our own deception will be unveiled.'

'Yes, sir.'

'Then we'll lock and bar the gates, trapping the Frogs inside and keeping the others out. I'm hoping that they will surrender, but we must be prepared for a nasty fight. Colonel Tate may have left his best men to guard the gates. I'll speak to Major Yates. I suggest two men to haul the ladder up, don't want them sneaking behind us. Arthur,' he said, turning to the boy, 'you stay here and keep out of sight.' He didn't wait for the boy's reply. 'Right, Sergeant, let's get this done."

'Yes, sir.'

Pritchard went into the barracks while Rosser's duty was to bring the rest of the Volunteers from the camp and into the stronghold. Mullone hunted the browncoats for any signs of trouble, but none paid either men any attention. *This is working*, he told himself. Soon the enemy would be prisoners, or dead, and that would leave Tate stranded. Perhaps in the futility, he might even surrender. And that would leave De Marin at a disadvantage. Tate's surrender would cause this foray to crumble, and Mullone would go after De Marin. Knowing how wily he was, Mullone knew he would have to be quick to catch him.

It was with those thoughts that Mullone heard a raised angry voice. It was coming from the barracks, and a tight knot clenched his stomach. He stepped out of the shadows and saw Pritchard and a dozen redcoats spilling out into the courtyard. But who was shouting?

'Who ordered you to form up?' A thickset officer was asking Pritchard, whose round face was reddening.

Mullone assumed this must be Yates. 'Major Yates,' Mullone said, approaching the man with a warming smile, 'may I have a word with you in private?'

Pritchard looked relieved.

Yates's face creased as he searched for some recognition of the voice and found none. He saw an unfamiliar officer coming towards him, and his demeanour went from ire to apprehension in an instant. 'Who the devil are you?' he croaked.

'Major Mullone, Lord Lovell's Dragoons.'

Yates threw a look towards the browncoats, the gates, then back to the Irishman. 'What are you doing here without my permission?'

'Might we talk in private?' Mullone asked again, this time not so mildly.

'You march in here a complete stranger,' Yates said sounding nervous. 'Do you have the relevant papers? No? My corporal tells me you ordered the men out of the barracks. May I ask why?' He then appeared more in control of the situation, because Mullone had chosen to be silent, and Yates assumed he had suppressed the Irishman with an authoritative tone. 'There is military etiquette and such like. There are rules, and these men are under my command. No one commands them but me. This is most peculiar. How did you get in? I should have you detained and arrested for—'

'You will do no such thing, sir!' Mullone suddenly erupted, and Yates shuddered from the harshness. 'You will allow your Volunteers to continue their duties.'

'I think y—'

'Be quiet!'

A bead of sweat ran down Yates's face. He peered at the redcoats who were forming up in two lines facing the gates. The French were looking his way.

Mullone noticed a sudden harsh resolve fix upon the Welshman's face.

'*Nous sommes découvert*!' Yates blurted out. '*Saissisez vos fusils et tuez-les*! *Maintenant*!'

Mullone understood the words and thumped Yates hard in the belly. The major doubled over and vomited. Mullone twisted to Pritchard and yelled, 'Corporal, look out! Make ready!'

A blast of musketry threw down six redcoats before they could level their primed weapons. One Welshman rolled on the ground, and another clawed at his uniform to inspect the damage, gasped, then fell back dead.

The long barrels wavered slightly as the redcoats were not accustomed to aiming with the heavy bayonets slotted. Pritchard, hit in the arm, staggered but managed to send a volley into the French as they charged through the powder smoke. A dozen of the enemy plunged into the redcoats with bayonet-tipped muskets, hard and fast, hitting like a prize-fighter's first blow, ready to follow the first with another attack and then another until the Volunteers were too dazed to do anything. They could rip the heart of the Welsh within minutes, and Mullone knew if they were defeated, the fort was lost.

'Volunteers! Volunteers!' Mullone shouted the word like a battle-cry before charging into the mêlée. A Frenchman, wearing the distinctive horsehair cap, was half-shrouded by the musket smoke, and Mullone thrust his sword hard into his chest. He withdrew it in time to meet two assailants who emerged from the reeking fog. He hissed at them like an angry cat, and his long blade flashed orange from the braziers' guttering light. The first man, a moustached NCO whose muscles strained the seams of his coat, rammed his bayonet at Mullone, who swept the oiled steel aside with his sword, then dodged as the second man stabbed forward. Mullone back swung and the blade sliced across the man's throat, sending a spurt of blood into the air.

A musket fired, but it was impossible to tell which side had fired the shot. A redcoat was knocked to the ground and gave a shrill yell as a bayonet plunged into his guts; the enemy grunted and ripped the blade free before slamming it into the dying man's neck. A redcoat with stubby limbs, appearing at Mullone's left flank, stamped his feet forward, jabbing his bayonet with practised skill, screaming and cursing the NCO in Welsh. The Frenchman with the pointed moustache edged backwards from the threat. Corporal Pritchard stumbled in front of Mullone, moaning and bleeding heavily from where a musket ball had splintered a rib. Mullone momentarily helped him aside, his sword arm blocked. Then the short Volunteer slipped on blood and the NCO was joined by two more comrades, and suddenly the bayonets stabbed and chopped into the Welshman before coming up, red and spattered with gore. Mullone stepped back and twisted left to right. Another redcoat was down, shot through the bowel, and three more were nervously withdrawing to the barracks.

'Press them back!' Mullone roared over the noise of the musket-fire, but the Volunteers around him were hesitating from fear, he'd seen it skittering in their eyes. 'Press them! Quickly now! We can do this!' The men held, checked by his command.

Mullone saw men running along the foot of the walls to climb the parapets to gain the advantage of height, and more were closing in and around the gates. Their browncoats looked black in the gloom. He swore. The enemy was winning this fight.

In the courtyard, men were fighting and dying, kicking and punching and clawing and biting. This was a gutter brawl between men having learned their skills in a hard life and desperation. The French, by experience, were pressing the part-time British soldiers backwards.

Muskets coughed and a Volunteer staggered backwards, his face wet with blood. The French NCO shouted commands at his men here to charge, but then his head snapped back, a ball having gone through an eye. Mullone jumped forward, lunged and smashed a bayonet aside as the man hauled on the trigger. The noise was huge, but Mullone swung his sword into the Frenchman's face, heard the scream and wrenched the blade free. A Frenchman with a scarred nose tried to grab his sword arm as another attempted to bayonet him, but Mullone tore himself free and hit the man in the face with the guard of the sword. The enemy went down with a bloodied nose. Mullone wasn't able to bring his sword around to defend his body as the long blade sliced at him. He managed to twist as the bayonet pierced his coat, ripping it and his uniform jacket underneath. The Frenchman cursed him, and Mullone smelled tobacco on his breath.

Shots sounded in the courtyard. Mullone knew they were from behind him. Ramrods rattled in fouled barrels. A man screamed somewhere. More shouts echoed from the gates, but Mullone couldn't risk a look that way and hoped the Volunteers held them. The Frenchman was stalking him and then Cadoc's carbine flamed, and the man disappeared into the drifting powder bank. Then there were no more enemies in front, and Mullone turned to a knot of redcoats who were loading muskets. 'Shoot them!' he pointed his sword, sticky with blood, towards three Frenchmen climbing to the parapets.

The Volunteers shouldered their weapons and sent a volley up at the men. One was hit in the spine and toppled backwards onto the ground. The other two were unhurt and were still clambering when Mullone ran after them like a hound scenting a fox. They turned and ran to the northwest bastion. Mullone put the point of his sword into the scabbard and then thrust the blade home so he could ascend.

Men were shouting and muskets banged below. He reached the parapet and searched the shadows for enemies. Mullone tugged free his sword and ran to the citadel, which contained two of the nine-pounders and the union flag. Then one of the Frenchmen stepped out into the flickering half-light, cocking his musket. Mullone screamed as he slammed into the man before he could level the firearm and pushed him shrieking over the battlements and down headfirst onto the hard ground below. The enemy's stock had thumped Mullone's cheek hard, and he shook his head to clear the pain. He rushed along the eastern ramparts as the enemy was taking aim at the redcoats below. His boots pounded on the stone, but he would not reach his prey in time.

'Look out!' Mullone yelled desperately.

Cadoc turned lightning fast, carbine to shoulder and put a bullet in the man.

Mullone stopped, panted and then took the risk of breaking an ankle as he jumped down onto the courtyard. He landed firmly and ran on towards the gates, sword held high. Mullone saw that Yates had gone, but that was of no concern right now. 'With me! All of you! To the gates!' Mullone bellowed at the redcoats, which spurred them to follow.

A Frenchman was crawling and Mullone kicked him in the face. Another, bayonet in hand, tried to slash it across Mullone's eyes, but the man didn't see the sword come up and gave a horrible mewing sound as the blade pierced his belly. Mullone twisted it free and the blood spilled like water onto his boots.

Rosser must be here soon, Mullone thought as he sprinted. *Please God be it Rosser who arrives at the gates first, and not Tate.*

The fight was even more desperate now because the French had clustered around the gates and barred them. There were a dozen of them remaining, bayonets fixed like a hedge of steel, and they would not give in. There were curses and challenges in French and in Welsh. The Volunteers fired a puny volley that splintered the air full of grunts and screams and moans. Out of the muzzles leapt flickering tongues of fire, and the leaden balls smashed into the enemy, killing three of the browncoats. One Volunteer shot his ramrod by mistake, the iron rod spun through the air. There were redcoats on the parapets, and they fired into the knot of Frenchmen from above.

'Charge them!' Mullone urged, pushing Volunteers into a ragged line. 'We can only win this when the scum are dead! Charge bayonets!'

The Welshmen advanced, and suddenly the large gates behind thumped. Two Frenchmen began to lift the bar. Mullone's heart felt as though it had plunged into freezing water. The gates would open, and more assailants would pour into the courtyard. Tate was here, and the realisation was terrible, damning and overwhelming.

The enemy had won!

'We must not let them open the gates!' Mullone barked, thinking that he must redouble his efforts.

Then Mullone heard a score of shouts outside and the distinctive sounds of Welsh. Rosser! He turned to the Volunteers, the joy of victory now within their grasp. 'For God and for Wales! Kill them!'

The redcoats leaped forward, screaming hatred.

The French died hard and did not break ranks to flee. The Volunteers lost six more men, but as the last enemy was struck on the back of the skull with the butt of a musket and bayoneted, Mullone helped raise the locking bar.

'Jesus bloody God,' Rosser gasped upon entering the courtyard, and flinched at the blood on Mullone's face, coat and sword. The rest of the Volunteers, eager to see the carnage, hurried through the large gates. Lieutenant Nash, hand to his mouth, could not take the stench and the blood and vomited.

'Good to see you, Sergeant,' Mullone said, chest heaving like a blown horse. 'My God, it is good to see you and your boys. Did you see the enemy out there?'

'No, sir, but he would have heard the fight. So would all the people of Fishguard and Goodwick.'

'Good and well.' Mullone watched the Volunteers strip the enemy dead of loot and herd three unwounded browncoats away. There were a further four wounded and ten Volunteers, and Rosser ordered them into carts to be escorted to Fishguard, where a retired naval surgeon lived. Tears pricked at the sergeant's eyes when he told Mullone the number of Welsh casualties. 'Seventeen dead. Seventeen families have lost a son, brother or husband.'

Mullone, drinking water from a canteen, looked sombre. 'I'm sorry, Sergeant. They did their duty well.'

Rosser had been shaking and tried to stop it by straightening. 'Yes, sir.'

Mullone peeked up at the barracks. 'Major Yates is in there,' he murmured.

Rosser gritted his teeth. 'Then we'll just have to prise him out like a cockle in a shell, sir.'

Mullone had the gates locked to prevent Tate coming, doubled the sentries and ordered Rosser and four privates to assist him. They entered the barracks and climbed the steps to find the door to the officers' quarters locked. Mullone knew it would be and rapped on the door with the pommel of his sword. 'Yates!' he called.

There was no answer. There was no sound at all coming from the room.

'Yates!' Mullone called again, this time banging the door louder, but still no answer. He put his head to the wood.

There was a heavy click, like a gun being cocked.

'Yates, for the love of God,' Mullone implored, 'the fort is in our hands now! You've lost! But there's no need for more violence!'

There was still no reply or further sound.

'Let's talk this through, Yates,' Mullone said and whispered for Rosser and two privates to shoot the lock with their muskets. He stepped back. 'I'm coming in to talk!'

There was no reply, so Mullone dipped his head at the sergeant. The three soldiers pulled back the hammers and, on the count of three, blasted the lock apart. Mullone stepped closer and gave the door a massive kick. It swung open.

Yates was sitting with a pistol to his head. His arm was rigid, but his face was contorting from a mixture of emotions.

There were no lights in the spacious room, just a soft red glow from a dying hearth. Mullone could smell stale cigar smoke and waved Rosser and the privates to stay back. 'We need to talk, Major,' he said calmly, moving carefully into the room. Maps and pieces of parchment littered the table. Vital information that Mullone needed and yet, strangely, Yates had not thought to tip the lot into the flames. His nose suddenly pricked at the copper tang of blood in the air.

'There's nothing you can say that will stop me from pulling this trigger,' Yates said.

'Fair enough,' Mullone said evenly.

Yates was not expecting that reply. 'I mean it!' he snarled.

'I know you do,' Mullone said, eyes lifting from the stained blanket on the floor. He looked into Yates's eyes; the sputtering red illumination gave the Welshman an almost demonic look. 'Is that where you murdered your captain?'

Yates's mouth twitched. 'He . . . I did not want to. He was asking too many questions. Too many . . .'

'So he was killed in order for you to keep your wee deception safe.'

'Yes,' Yates said feebly.

'Did you do the deed, or was it your friend, Tate?'

Yates swallowed hard. 'I did,' he said eventually.

Mullone rested himself against the table, less than four feet away from Yates. 'Convinced yourself that it was the right thing to do?' Yates didn't answer him. 'You must have some remorse about murdering one of your own officers? No? No compunction whatsoever to having killed an officer, a friend and a fellow Welshman? No? Really? You'd have to have a heart as cold as ice not to have any feelings about doing such a thing here in Fishguard, of all places!'

'It had to be done,' Yates mumbled.

Mullone saw his pistol hand quiver and noticed that Yates's left arm hung limp at his side. 'There is never an excuse for murder,' Mullone retorted with a sharp scowl. 'How long have you been working for the French?'

Again, Yates said nothing. The fire crackled and spat a glowing ember onto the stone floor, where it fizzed a trail of smoke before dying out.

'Were you on our side during the war against the enemy?'

Yates gave a ghost of a smile. 'What side would that be?'

'The side fighting against King George's enemies,' Mullone replied. 'An oath you took when you became a soldier and an officer of the British Army.'

'When you are young, it is very easy to become disillusioned and corrupted.'

'Did Tate corrupt you?'

Yates's trigger finger flexed.

'You knew Tate back then, yes?' Mullone probed further. 'Back all those years to that bloody war. I was there, you know. I was young, like you. I saw terrible things: friends and loved ones die.'

Mullone sighed heavily and rested his sword, caked with blood, onto the table facing to the right yet still gripped the hilt. Yates's eyes skimmed over it. 'Were you a spy?'

The Welshman was silent. Something in his face said yes.

'So you were.' Mullone paused. 'Just think, if we had won the war, we'd have had to impose ourselves further on the colonists by means of force,' he said as though he was pondering the thought. 'Flex our muscles in the heavy-handed way we British always seem to do. Impose more taxes with cold steel and bullets. That doesn't sound good to me. No. I think it was probably better that we lost that war, don't you? It might well have saved so many more lives.' Mullone looked around the room, eyes resting on the form underneath several blankets on one of the half-dozen cots near the far wall. His mouth instantly went rigid knowing that was the captain. His green eyes narrowed. 'Tell me why you turned your coat and betrayed your country?'

A strange laugh erupted out of the corner of Yates's mouth. 'I was shown the true path to Enlightenment,' he said. 'I became one of the virtuous farmers, merchants and fishermen that won independence from the corrupt and greedy British. I betrayed nothing.'

'You're British!'

'I am a revolutionary, and I am free!'

Now it was Mullone's turn to laugh. 'You think you're free?'

'*Liberté, Egalité, Fraternité,*' Yates uttered.

'You are a slave, Major. No matter what you think or do, you are a slave. And the French revolutionaries have their own ideas on what liberty and democracy are.'

Yates brought the pistol around so the muzzle was pointed directly at Mullone's face. Rosser growled from the doorway, but Mullone shook his head.

'And you think you're free, my fine Irish friend?' Yates gave a mocking smile. 'I hear many stories from Ireland that speak of a great revolution to come. A revolution borne of blood and hatred. It will be catastrophic and terrifying.'

'I don't fear stories.'

'Ireland will soon be free from the English.'

'A few angry men do not constitute an uprising,' Mullone said evenly.

'A fire grows in the dark.'

Mullone sighed. 'All light casts shadows. Whatever happens in Ireland . . . well, they certainly don't need your French friends with their imbalanced and embittered ideals whispering out from the shadows. I'll tell you that the more they interfere, the harder the kicking they'll receive.'

Yates let out a long irritating laugh, then fingered the trigger without any real force.

'Before you shoot me,' Mullone said softly, 'would you enlighten me as to what Tate is doing here?'

Sweat streaked down Yates's maniacal face. 'I will say nothing on the matter. Only that tomorrow is a new dawn. Though for some, it will be the last time they wake to see a sunrise.'

Mullone blinked, bobbed his head and went to step away, then with lightning speed, whipped his sword hard above the table, slicing into the major's hand. The blow caused Yates to pull the trigger. The pistol thundered and the ball smacked into the stone wall with a thud. The attack had severed Yates's thumb, and he rocked in the chair, clutching his wound to his chest with his clumsy left arm, gasping and groaning pitifully. Dark blood spattered his coat, belts and breeches. The impotent pistol lay smoking on the floor along with the blood-soaked digit.

Mullone brought the sword to Yates's face. 'You are a coward and a murderer,' he said.

'Go to hell!'

Mullone lowered his sword arm closer so that the tip prodded Yates's throat, pricking flesh and drawing blood. 'You are going to tell me everything I want to know.'

Yates's eyes and mouth shook with defiance.

Mullone pressed the blade harder.

'Don't kill me!' The Welshman suddenly quaked; spittle twirled between his lips. 'I'll tell you everything, just don't kill me!'

Mullone leaned in closer, his eyes revealing inner menace. 'I'm not going to kill you, Yates, but I'm going to kill someone else.'

And so Yates, petrified and in pain, talked.

Once Mullone was satisfied that the major had spoken the truth and exhausted himself, Yates was escorted away under guard, and Mullone was directed to the Woolwich gunners. There were four of them, all invalids and commanded by a bombardier called Carter. He was a likeable man, thin, with scars deforming the left side of his face, neck and hand. He scratched with dirty nails at the horror of twisted pink skin that had once been his cheek. Carter told Mullone how he had been part of a gun-team serving in the American Colonies when a rebel shot had hit the ammunition wagon, causing it to explode in a fiery burst next to him. The rest of his team had died, but Carter had survived. He was invalided out of the army and found work for a time in Woolwich's Royal Brass Foundry, manufacturing cannon. 'Sweated in the moulding pits, and even now I can still hear the hammering, the filing, the chiselling and the stamping,' he happily told Mullone, who tried to imagine the heat from the molten iron as it was poured into the great moulds. Carter spoke enthusiastically, but awkwardly because his mouth was drawn tight on his left side. 'They thought I might hate the sight of the fires, on account of what happened to me, but I was happy, see. The more guns we made, the more of our enemies would likely be killed. Got my own back, see.'

'I want you to fire one of your guns, no ammunition, just prime it,' Mullone told him. 'No need to waste shot.'

"Tis a good job, sir, on account of us only having three rounds stored in the magazine.'

Mullone gaped. 'Three?'

'Yes, sir,' Carter answered as they strode towards the northwest bastion. 'We've not had the supplies in.'

'Lucky that we didn't need your guns to defend the fort,' Mullone said, noticing that two of the gunners limped.

Carter smiled knowingly, which didn't do anything to enhance his features, making them mocking and open to abuse. 'Lucky indeed, sir.'

The eight nine-pounders were actually naval guns, mounted on wooden naval carriages, and fired shot weighing nine pounds, each shot propelled by three pounds of gunpowder. The guns were supported on a wooden firing platform; ropes and train-tackle were anchored to the stone embrasures. Each gun was restrained by thick breeching ropes lashed to keep it from recoiling out of the bastion. The train-tackle was used to run the fired gun on its squat wooden wheels back into position.

Carter ordered the Woolwich gunners in their bluecoats to prepare to fire the cannon. Mullone watched as a nominated gunner pushed a bag and a cloth wad down the barrel with a ramrod. Carter then thrust a metal pricker into the touchhole to rip into the powder bag. The gunners then ran the cannon with the ropes so that the barrel pointed out of the gun embrasure. Carter poured a little finer powder from a powder horn down into the touchhole to prime it. When he was happy with the gun's position, although it didn't matter as it wasn't loaded or even being aimed, Carter hauled back the hammer, a flintlock mechanism similar but heavier to that of a musket, to half-cock. He spun around to Mullone.

'Gun ready, sir,' he said. 'I would stand back and cover your ears as well, sir.'

'Ready when you are,' Mullone answered when he had complied.

'Thank you, sir.' Carter made sure his team was well clear of the gun. He took in a lungful of air. 'Fire!' he shouted. Then, holding the lanyard, which was a long cord attached to the lock, he gave it a swift pull.

The lock snapped forward, and the cannon rent the night air with its roar. The recoil was slight, but the sound of the single gun seemed hugely loud, and the cloud of acrid smoke, caught by a brisk wind, enveloped half the fort's northern ramparts and shrouded the union flag. The gunshot faded, then was echoed back from the shore before fading a second time.

Mullone looked west across the valley towards Carreg Wastad. At the top of the heights, a number of lights flickered and glowed through trees and the rocks. Enemy campfires.

The wind whisked the rill of smoke away from the bastion, and Mullone gazed up at the flag.

He breathed a sigh of relief.

The cannon had bellowed a signal to the world that Fishguard Fort was safe.

The Second Day

Thursday, 23rd February, 1797

It was still dark when Mullone woke.

He had managed to snatch three hours' sleep and now peered out from one of the windows in the officers' quarters to where the deadly clash had occurred. There had been no rain in the night, and patches of blood showed like the spillage of paint in the braziers' light. Vickers had been taken away with the Welsh dead to the small church of Saint Mary's to be buried. The wounded had also gone in carts; the French dead lay in a pile outside the walls until it was decided what to do with them. Some of the villagers had come up to see what had happened, and Mullone sent Cadoc home with them.

Mullone squinted up at the ominous clouds, which were the same colour as the hills. Rosser had brought him a mug of tea, a hunk of bread and some salted pork. Something scratched in the rafters. A mouse, perhaps. Or a bird on the rooftop.

'You should sleep some more, sir,' the sergeant said, his own eyes puffy and bloodshot.

'Are you telling me this isn't a dream?'

Rosser smiled. 'Last night I prayed and dreamed of angels like St Brynach once did.' The sergeant then looked embarrassed. He fiddled with a loose button. 'Some of my men feel ashamed that they,' he paused to think carefully what he was about to say, 'hesitated during the fight, sir. They wanted me to tell you that they feel ashamed of their conduct. They aren't chicken-hearted.'

The Volunteers were part-time soldiers, and they had faced better men, but Mullone was not going to say that the Welshmen were really enthusiastic amateurs. 'Your men fought admirably, Sergeant,' he said truthfully, knowing that a large proportion had never seen battle before. They had not seen what horror a musket ball or steel blade could do to a man. 'Some of them are not even twenty. I probably would have done the same thing if it were me. Tell them they did their duty, and that's all that matters.'

Rosser looked reassured. 'Thank you, sir. What will happen to the major now?'

Mullone swallowed a mouthful of pork, feeling his cheekbone ache from when the stock had hit him. He rubbed it and felt a slight swelling. 'He'll be kept under guard with the prisoners until it is decided where to send them. There's a prison in Pembroke, isn't there?'

'Yes, sir, the Golden Prison,' Rosser answered with a scowl, then brightened. 'I could have an accident with a musket, sir?'

Mullone smiled at the thought. 'Let him face his court-martial, Sergeant. Let the craven bugger squirm.'

'For what he's done, sir, it isn't enough.'

Mullone agreed, but Yates's fate was sealed. And there were more things to worry about now. Tate had not made an appearance in the early hours, and Lieutenant Samuel Nash had ridden out to give Mullone's report to Colonel Knox. Mullone was now reading the scrap of paper the worried lieutenant, now acting as Knox's aide, had returned with.

Major,
I strongly impress you, with all haste, to evacuate with the utmost rapidity. I have commanded Lieutenant Nash to order the remaining Volunteers to march with all equipment and arms to Fishguard. I have the Newport Volunteers at hand and have received word that Lord Cawdor is bringing up a large body of reserves. I would imagine by midday we will receive orders from our superiors to strike against the enemy in full.
I have given the gunners permission to spike the guns for fear that the enemy will likely use them against us.

Yours,
Colonel T. Knox

Mullone was almost tempted to throw the letter into the fire. He drained his mug and went outside to find an ashen-faced Nash waiting in the saddle.

'It's just us two who'll be leaving,' Mullone told him as he rammed his helmet on his head. 'The guns and the Volunteers will continue to hold this fort.'

Nash shuddered, then looked up at the defences. 'That won't sit well with the colonel, sir,' he said resignedly, then scratched violently at his neck. He was sure he'd been bitten by a louse in his tent. He hated sleeping outdoors, yet the thought of staying in the barracks appalled him after what had happened. He'd even shown Sergeant Rosser the red itchy mark that morning, but the NCO had just chuckled.

'You been keeping a girl in your cot, sir?' Rosser had asked innocently.

Nash had blushed. 'No, I have not!'

'Oh, I see, sir. Well, if it wasn't Pastor Huw Penry's daughter, Tegan, then it must have been a louse.' Rosser had taken a closer inspection of the tiny wound.

'It was a louse,' Nash had insisted.

Rosser had sniffed. 'Better put it in the books, sir.'

'Books?' Nash had said, confused.

'Casualty list, sir. The poor little louse is probably dead now.' The older man had started to laugh and Nash was left humiliated.

'Colonel Knox doesn't take kindly to advice or to disagreement, sir,' Nash pointed out, getting back to the matter at hand and hoping the Irish major would take heed of his warning.

Mullone spared Nash a pitying glance and climbed up onto Yates's saddled bay horse. He gave the young man a wide smile of sublime confidence. 'That's why I'm coming with you.'

The two men rode out across the isthmus and joined the road that cut its way south like a scar through the wind-driven land towards Fishguard. The hooves clattered noisily on the village's main street, but not a soul met them. It looked deserted.

71

'Where is everyone? Where is the colonel?' Mullone asked.

'He left orders that Fishguard is to be abandoned, sir,' Nash replied uncomfortably.

Mullone turned slowly. 'He's done what?' he said, astonished.

Nash looked as though he didn't believe what he had just said either. 'Colonel Knox said that the enemy would likely seize the village because of the value of the harbour and fort and so thought it prudent to pull everyone back, perhaps to Pembroke or Haverfordwest.' He shook his head glumly. 'One of the girls has gone into labour, and Llewellyn's dog is missing.' He looked around. 'It's not my place to say so, sir, but it has caused a panic.'

Mullone rubbed his forehead. 'I'm not surprised. He's taken it upon himself to frighten the folk. Where have they gone?'

'I think most have stayed put, to be honest. Most of the people here are stubborn and . . .'

Nash's voice stopped because there was a sudden commotion at the end of the street, and Mullone could see people milling about. He jerked the horse towards the crowd, where they appeared to be armed with pitchforks, axes, hoes and knives. They were surging west.

Nash saw a girl amongst the men and boys. 'Tegan! What are you doing?' he called over the din.

The girl, wearing a sombre dress underneath her coat, looked up and smiled at him. 'We're off to show these Frenchies that we won't be cowed!' She saw Mullone and curtsied.

Mullone offered a grim nod back, then cast an eye over the heaving throng armed for battle. There was a woman wrapped in a shawl, waddling like a fattened duck. 'Where do you think you'll go now?' he called out to them.

'Where the French are, Colonel,' Tegan replied, not knowing Mullone's rank. 'We've seventeen brave men from this village to avenge!'

A ripple of cheers erupted. Fists and weapons punched the air.

'The French have weapons!' Mullone said, his voice climbing in pitch. 'They have swords, pistols and muskets! Leave the fighting to the soldiers!'

A man spat a curse in Welsh, and one of the fishermen, with scales glinting in his dark beard, roared and chanted death to the *lladron,* Welsh for brigands and thieves.

Tegan laughed, her eyes vivid and large. 'We're not waiting for no one, Colonel! Begw said she will cut a Frenchman from ear to ear with her fish knife, and Old Non said she will take a pair of shears and castrate them!'

'Thieves? What have the French taken? What have they done?' Nash asked, baffled, but the folk were striding away. 'Tegan!' he called, his voice now hoarse, but the girl did not look around.

'I blame your colonel for this,' Mullone grunted. 'There are no soldiers guarding the village either.' He fell silent and then swore under his breath.

'Sir?'

'Let's find him,' Mullone glowered, 'for I have a few choice words to say to the man.'

Thomas Knox, Nash explained to Mullone as they trailed the rabble west, was appointed colonel of the Fishguard and Newport Volunteer Infantry due to the influence of his father, Sir William Knox. The commission had provided Thomas with an elevated position in the Pembrokeshire society, but some men refused to serve posts within the Volunteers due to the apparent nepotism and the fact that he had no combat experience. Knox had the habit of keeping his commission on his person at all times because many people repudiated that he was a colonel and renounced his insistence on addressing him with that rank.

The land became steep, and Mullone saw a glint of colour in a stand of sycamores about a half-mile from the road. 'There he is, Lieutenant! On that hill!'

The hill was actually an ancient embankment, a grass-covered mound ringed with gorse and hawthorn bushes. Mullone and Nash left the road, galloping and jumping over the undergrowth, sending clods of earth into the air, up to where Knox and a half-dozen officers were scouring the western heights for enemies. Mullone thought Yates's horse was a bit docile and not as fast or disciplined as *Tintreach*, and he felt a sudden pang of longing to see his stallion again.

Sunlight filtered sluggishly over the land and promised to be a warm, clear day. Birds chirped from the trees.

'Ah, Lieutenant Nash,' Knox greeted him with a thin smile, though Mullone judged it was put on. 'I trust the men are on their way here and the guns have been spiked.'

Nash, looking faint, quivered. 'N-No, sir.'

Knox frowned, thinking he had not heard his aide correctly. 'No?'

The officers beside the young colonel had turned round to witness this act of impudence.

'They have not, sir,' Mullone answered instead.

An age seemed to pass before Tate replied. 'Since when does a major outrank a colonel?'

Mullone could already smell spirits on the man's breath. 'They don't, sir,' he replied, 'but common sense overrides ignorance.'

The words hung in the air between them.

One of the officers gasped, and another dropped his telescope.

Knox was livid, his thin face, already lined and aged through far too much alcohol, shook like a ship on violent seas. 'How dare you speak to me like that! How dare you countermand my orders! I'll have your brought before a tribunal for this outrage!' he simmered. 'Answer me this: what would happen if the Crapauds land more troops at Fishguard? Well? I'll tell you. They'll snatch the harbour and village and garrison the fort. Our guns will be used against us! We will lose more Welsh blood, or perhaps because you're a damned Paddy, you don't care!'

Mullone let the words fade before he made a soft clicking sound and the horse walked to Knox. The colonel stiffened at the movement.

'Listen to me, you prinked-up wee bastard,' Mullone said so that only Knox could hear, 'I'll not listen to another fuddled word from you. The guns and the fort are still in our hands. The French ship left to rejoin the fleet, and if you had garrisoned Fishguard and guarded the roads with picquets, you might well have captured the enemy commander, a Colonel Tate, who had been stranded when your men fought and died to protect the stronghold. Due to your lack of experience and understanding, you have allowed an enemy of great importance, and perhaps a chance to force their surrender, to simply

74

walk free, and where they most probably took the road past Goodwick to reunite with their host!' Mullone had spoken louder and angrier with each sentence and was unabashed at speaking to a colonel this way.

Knox gulped, knowing he had made a fatal error but was not going to admit that he had spent the night gambling and drinking with the officers from the Newport's division of the regiment. Then there was that fumble with the serving girl with the big bubbies. He cleared his throat and tried to steady his thoughts.

When Mullone spoke, his voice throbbed again with anger. 'You sit there and ask whether the guns were spiked and the fort abandoned? You dishonour your men, sir!' He stopped to catch a breath. 'You have instilled panic in the village and a mob has armed themselves with whatever they could get their hands on and are marching,' he jerked a hand behind him, 'up that road to exact vengeance. If any of them are killed, Colonel,' he said the last word sourly, 'then their deaths are on your conscience.'

Knox didn't know what to say to that; he just cleared his throat again, his eyes swivelling as though he was pondering how to contain the situation. He twisted in the saddle. 'Captain Nisbett!' he called, then had to shout louder because his voice was cracked.

The rangy man appeared after a moment from the foot of the hill, waving his stick at Mullone in recognition. 'Morning, Major.'

'Morning, Captain,' Mullone replied.

'I have to commend you on the defence of the fort,' Nisbett said, tottering up to Mullone and extending his hand. 'Everyone is talking about it. You're a damned hero.'

Mullone took the proffered hand and shook it. 'The Volunteers are the heroes. I merely aided and tried not to get in the way.'

'Quite, quite,' Nisbett said, experience telling him that Mullone was a good officer and was probably belittling his own gallantry. Nisbett was about to add a comment and realised the air was still thick with the lasting breath of wrath.

'I have appointed Captain Nisbett as commander of the Fishguard Volunteer Scouts,' Knox proclaimed, gripped with a sudden fervour. 'They are to probe the enemy and locate their positions. He has experience of this type of warfare.'

Mullone, tempted to reply that Knox was a cod-headed dullard and was not up to the task of appointing anything, nodded assent. 'A wise decision,' he said.

Knox's head bobbed. 'I thought so too.' He looked down at Nisbett. 'Major Mullone has not spiked the guns and the Fishguard Volunteers now hold the fort.'

'A wise decision, sir,' Nisbett echoed, giving Mullone a mischievous wink.

'I still think we should consolidate at Haverfordwest,' Knox remarked aloud, not giving up on his idea.

No one offered an answer. Mullone's eyes traversed the high bank, past the hawthorn bushes studded with berries, to where redcoats were stretched out beside a wide patch of marshland. Mullone considered these were the men from Newport, and they were guarding a small footbridge and a much larger bridge to the north near a tranquil wood of beech and yew trees, where streams and brooks bled into the ground. There were redcoats in loose order far across the swamp to the west, Nisbett's men, but Mullone knew the real difficulty was the rocky heights. They blocked views of the swathes of moorland, fields and scattered homesteads, but more importantly, the French positions.

As if reading Mullone's thoughts, Nisbett made a suggestion. 'I think I should take the Scouts up to the elevated ground for a better look at the enemy. Find out where the buggers are.'

Knox busied himself with the ridge, silent-mouthed, and with a sulky air about him.

'With your permission, Colonel?' Nisbett pressed.

Knox turned his gaze slowly, forcing himself to be cordial. 'Of course, Captain.'

'Thank you, sir,' Nisbett said cheerfully. 'Time to do the king's work and send these Frogs back to hell!'

Just then, as the veteran departed to issue orders and Mullone was about to enquire after *Tintreach*, a voice called from the road and Mullone saw that two horsemen were approaching. The leading rider was a strongly built man wearing a cloak over a scarlet coat with bright blue facings, gold buttons and lace. He had a lean face, thoughtful eyes and the air of a true soldier about him. The second horseman was perhaps nineteen or twenty years old with an aloof expression that reminded Mullone of Knox.

'Colonel Colby!' Knox greeted the officer with the blue facings stiffly.

'Colonel Knox,' Colby responded equally as laboriously. 'This is my aide, the Honourable Captain William Edwardes,' he announced.

'Pleasure.' Knox dipped his head at Edwardes. 'I have had the honour of meeting your father. A forthright man, if there ever was, but a man with a vast measure of intellect. Please pass on my regards to him.'

If Edwardes was pleased by the meeting, he didn't show it. He was the son of Lord William Edwardes, 1st Baron Kensington and MP for Haverfordwest, and already renowned for being a loutish womaniser. He glared at the assembled officers with impatience, as though he was being kept from something important.

Colby, the commanding officer of the Pembrokeshire Militia, gawped at Mullone, trying to place him, but failed.

Mullone pre-empted the introduction. 'Major Lorn Mullone, sir, Lord Lovell's Dragoons.'

'A little way from home, Mullone?' Colby said, bemused.

'I have that in common with the French, sir,' Mullone replied, to which the colonel smiled.

'The major works for the government,' Knox said. 'He is the one who spotted the French ships at anchor and warned the locals so that they managed to escape with minor mishap. It is my estimation that the major saved many lives.'

Mullone, astonished at the candour, gave Knox a slight bow in the saddle, who returned his gesture with a syrupy smirk.

Colby gave Mullone an approving look. 'I know of you,' he revealed. 'An old companion of mine, Tom Nisbett, sent word to me that the French had landed and had corroborated the fact with you in Fishguard.'

'He did, sir.'

'Captain Nisbett is now commander of my Scouts,' Knox announced haughtily.

Colby switched his stare to the young colonel, and Mullone saw his expression darken. 'Where are they now?' he enquired sharply.

Knox shrugged and swept an arm limply towards the rank marshy terrain. 'I hope your presence here doesn't mean that you are commandeering my men?' His timbre was icy.

'On the contrary,' Colby uttered, 'I came in person to tell you that Lord Cawdor is now marching with infantry, cavalry and artillery from Haverfordwest.'

'I have already been appraised of that,' Knox replied snootily. 'However, they won't get here until this evening,' he added begrudgingly.

'They are marching as fast as they can,' Colby countered. 'Lord Cawdor thought it wise to emplace more guns at Haverfordwest Castle with artillery brought from the Royal Navy in case of vastly superior numbers. Captain Longcroft has ordered the crew from a cutter to dismount their guns and bring up a battery with sailors. There is the Castlemartin Troop of the Pembroke Yeomanry Cavalry, the Cardiganshire Militia and the Pembroke Volunteer Infantry. As you will find, gentlemen,' Colby said optimistically, 'we have a sizeable force on its way here. More will come once the call is answered.'

'A little too late,' Knox muttered loftily.

'I'm afraid it's still not enough, sir,' Mullone advised Colby.

'I fathom they have neither artillery nor horses.'

'Doubtful that they have any cavalry, but we don't know about cannon. They may have brought some from the ships, sir,' Mullone suggested.

'Hardly possible,' Knox snorted.

Mullone ignored him. 'They have had a full day to do what they want, and I fear the enemy is somewhere in the region of fifteen hundred strong.'

Colby seemed to be taken aback that news, but he could not show a lack of confidence, especially when most of the officers were young and raw. 'If and when the time comes,' he said in a voice that carried, 'that's when a soldier earns his pay. And the British soldier is a better soldier, and we'll kick their French arses all the way home!'

The Newport Volunteer officers cheered the sentiment; one even applauded.

'Well said,' Knox muttered through the corner of his mouth. 'There's still the matter of the prisoners,' he said petulantly.

'Prisoners?' Colby asked.

Knox hesitated because he had exposed what Mullone and his men had endured whilst he had been languid.

'Major Mullone and the Volunteers took possession of Fishguard Fort, sir,' Nash said, 'where they encountered a score of the enemy. I arrived late with my company from our billet to find there had been a dreadful fight within the walls. We suffered seventeen dead, and we took seven prisoners. Including Major Yates, who appears to have been working subversively with the French.'

Colby's eyes widened. He looked sideways at Edwardes, who glared back as though he suspected more traitors were present.

'My God, is this true?' Colby said. 'There was a traitor here?'

'Unfortunately, yes, sir,' Mullone responded.

'Colonel Knox requested the fort's guns to be spiked and the fort—' Nash blurted.

Knox cleared his throat loud enough to drown out Nash's voice. 'Thank you, Lieutenant!' He shot him a withering look. 'We have prisoners, Colonel.'

'I want them,' Colby said briskly, still wide-eyed. 'Lord Cawdor will want to see them.'

'He shall have them,' Knox said silkily.

Colby offered a curt smile. 'I will now report back to advise him of your preparations.'

Knox looked puzzled. 'Preparations?'

'The prisoners and your Scouts, Colonel,' Colby answered, as if speaking to a dim child. 'I want you to hold the Frogs back. Probe, but do not engage. You're vastly outnumbered. Wait for us.'

'Colonel—' Knox said, about to pour scorn on that advice.

'I suggest,' Colby interrupted with a stern voice, 'that you refrain from engaging the enemy until Lord Cawdor gives an order to the contrary. Is that understood?'

Knox ground his teeth and offered only a grunt as a reply.

'Good,' Colby replied. 'Good day to you, gentleman,' he offered a cordial nod at Mullone, before he and his aide wheeled their horses around and cantered south.

'God's teeth!' Knox exclaimed impatiently. 'We're to sit here and wait for the damned Crapauds to show themselves! We've a whole day to wait until Lord Cawdor arrives. Pah! This isn't soldiering!'

'I think it prudent to adhere to your orders, sir,' Mullone voiced.

Knox shot him a disparaging look and then stared sulkily at the heights.

No one said anything for what seemed an age, and Mullone, irritated by Knox's demeanour, did not want to strike up conversation, so he kicked Yates's mare downhill. The men of Newport made a break in their ranks for Mullone to pass through. The horse easily trotted through the marsh, creating ripples in the pools and scattering insects on the surfaces. A pheasant gave its crowing call from somewhere in the wood, and a redcoat tried to imitate it, causing a ripple of laughter. The horse's ears twitched, and she gave a low, throaty sound.

'There, there, girl,' Mullone said soothingly, sensing the horse's nervousness.

'Major Mullone,' Nisbett called out, touching his forelock. Ravens flapped from the peaks far beyond and down towards the treetops.

The quagmire gave way to a series of gentle rises that became steeper hills that swept north towards the great rocks of Garnwnda, where beyond were the farms and village of Llanwnda. That was where Mullone had seen the bright blush of the campfires against the sky. He thought about Father Bach and hoped the old priest was being treated well.

'No sign of the bastards,' Nisbett said, 'but I can feel them. My skin itches.'

Mullone looked along the screen of redcoats. 'And should they emerge, are the Scouts ready for them?'

'They are now,' Nisbett grinned.

They walked together. A sudden chill wind blew, making the air as sharp as cut glass, and Mullone was thankful for his greatcoat. Hedges and banks lined the road to his right that linked with the thoroughfare from Fishguard and up to Llanwnda.

'I know this place like the back of my hand, Major,' Nisbett said, no sign of his age or walking stick impeding his gait. 'A beautiful part of the world. In the spring, these hills are thick with carpets of pink thrift and white campion. The woods are full of deer and woodcock and the meadows call with the sounds of corncrakes and warblers.'

'Aye, reminds me of home,' Mullone said wistfully.

'And you'll go back after this?'

'That depends on the French.'

The old captain chuckled, then looked severe. 'Damn their nerve for coming here. We shall beat them at every turn!'

They climbed up to the series of green ridges, the Scouts manoeuvring like light infantry. With a good view of the road, Nisbett halted his temporary command. They were a little over a half mile away from where Knox still brooded. Mullone could see Fishguard and the harbour that resembled a shard of hammered silver against the dark land. If the French did attack now, Mullone thought, they would cut through Knox's men like a sword through a wine sack.

*

Colonel William Tate, finished his cup of coffee, ignored the people around him and got up from the chair. He paced over to the large window of the south-facing room and peered outside.

Trehowel Farm was a substantial smallholding of two buildings, both of local stone, well maintained and prosperous. There was even an herb garden that enjoyed the sunshine; not much there now, but in the soil there might be seeds of sage and thyme. The vegetable plot was already cultivated for lettuce, onions and tomatoes. He could smell the dung heap. It was a comfortable home, Tate mused, and he felt a pang of regret for commandeering it as his headquarters.

The owner, John Mortimer, was seated with his wife in the room, both nervous, and Tate could not look at them. Guilt and ignominy plagued his mind.

Le Brun had organised yesterday's landing very well, with the lead boat containing good, able soldiers from the Legion. It was early when the farmer, his wife and six workers had been captured without a struggle as they foolishly tried to load belongings onto a cart. The troops had then spread out to secure the other farms and reconnoitre while sixteen boatloads of men, arms and ammunition were brought ashore. One boat full of stores was lost in the surf, but there were no casualties. Le Brun had proved that he was a good organiser, but he had not registered the prospect of indiscipline despite knowing the fragile makeup of the Legion.

His men had broken windows, destroyed the pantry, emptied the cupboards of every scrap of food, slaughtered one of Mortimer's cows, damaged a wood carving, stolen cutlery and blankets and burned window frames, chairs, some barrels and a table for firewood. Having been content to set fire to gorse bushes and tore down old timber from a barn for more fires, Tate was riled. There was one crime that had been committed at the time when he had withdrawn his remaining men when the damned redcoats had somehow found out the ruse and secured the fort. A despicable crime, and he was about to confront the perpetrators.

Tate sighed heavily. The fire crackled loudly in the hearth. He turned sharply, and Mrs Mortimer took an intake of breath. He dropped his steady gaze and turned back to the window. A clock chimed nine o' clock.

'Please rest assured that no harm will come to the pair of you,' Tate said after the delicate peals had ended. 'I deeply apologise for this inconvenience, and I do hope our intrusion has not caused you a great deal of grief.'

'Your men have damaged my property,' Mortimer fumed, unable to control himself.

'Such things happen in war,' uttered one of the Frenchmen present.

Everyone looked at the speaker.

It was the French agent, De Marin, who stood along with six other officers in the room.

'Not only that,' Mortimer said, 'you are disrupting my farm. Where are my work-hands? What have you done with them?'

No one answered.

'I have ditches to clear, a new door for the barn to finish, hedging, carting .' He stopped when his wife tapped him forcefully on the leg.

'No one cares about your work,' De Marin said. 'This is war! Your daily toils are of no consequence to us.'

The officers looked to the American, who was still facing the window, to see his reaction. His reflection, to those that could see, showed a man who was pensive and yet detached.

'War, he muttered, as though he was pondering the notion of it. He sighed again and turned to his two Aides. '*Lieutenant* Faucon, *Lieutenant* L'Hanhard, with me,' he said, and left the room.

Tate turned right into a hallway, past a scullery and into the kitchen, where more officers gathered around a table. There was the unmistakeable smell of eggs and coffee. They stood to attention, but he ignored them. Outside, near the vegetable plot, he met with Lieutenant Marrock, who was cleaning his teeth with a sliver of wood. 'Come with me,' Tate ordered in English, because the freckled lieutenant did not speak French, and the four men sauntered down a path towards a thatched, open building where carts and other farm wagons were housed. Dirty straw covered the floor. An officer was seated on a barrel. There were six privates, with bayonets fixed, appearing to guard two men hunched against the far wall. The officer, Le Brun, a slim, neat man with manicured hands, rose to his feet, and the guardsmen stood to rigid attention. Tate waved them down. He paced into the edifice, stooping under the lintels. The two men watched his approach with disdain.

Tate browsed the cobweb-haunted rafters above, then dropped his steely gaze to the prisoners. '*Fusilier* Pett, *Fusilier* Wagnon, you are accused of the rape of a local girl.' His face was grim. 'Not only did you break into the family's home and assault her, but you attacked her female companion and discharged your musket, wounding that girl as they both tried to flee. Thankfully, they have been treated by *Chirurgien* Larand and are being looked after. He managed to extract the ball and,' he winced as he imagined the girl's torment at the hands of these two men, 'to treat their other wounds. What do you have to say for yourselves? Speak up!'

One of prisoners, lank-haired and bearded, spat to show his contempt. The other man, blue-eyed and strikingly handsome, was silent.

'*Fusilier* Pett,' Tate addressed the good-looking one, 'your conduct besmirches your once excellent career. I am told you have served the Republic for four years. A steady man, but last year you were stripped of your promotion to *corporel* for drunken behaviour.' The prisoner offered no reply to that charge. Tate looked at the bearded one; the thick, matted hair hid a collection of scars. '*Fusilier* Wagnon, there is nothing good to say about your character. You are a convicted murderer, released from your bonds and into the Legion. Mistakenly, your chains were unlocked on the voyage over. That was an error.' He couldn't stop himself from glancing at Le Brun. 'My error,' he announced. 'And I have to correct that.' Tate half-turned to the officers. 'Faucon, your blade,' he instructed.

'Sir?' The *lieutenant* asked, confused.

'Your sword,' Tate said gruffly.

Faucon unsheathed his sword and turned it so Tate was offered the hilt first.

'What are you doing, sir?' Le Brun asked.

Tate's face hardened. 'Be quiet.'

The American faced the villains and tossed the slim blade onto the straw. They stared back mutely.

'Soldiers should die with a weapon in their hand,' Tate answered. 'If you beat me, you shall rejoin the ranks. If you don't, you will die like the animals that you are.'

'Sir! You can't—' Le Brun started to say.

'Quiet!' Tate spat.

The two rapists hung back.

'Fight!' Tate roared at them. 'Fight, you bastards!'

There was a moment of incomprehensible silence.

Wagnon sprang forward, quicker than Tate could have imagined, and drew back a fist. Tate stepped back and was withdrawing his sword when the punch came at him. He dodged, and the blade rasped free. Wagnon charged, threw another this time his left and Tate ducked away. The rapist, snarling, took another swing, but Tate blocked the fist with his left arm and, in a rage caused by their heinous actions, slashed his sword at the man's neck. The blade bit home, Tate sawed it, and blood sprayed high. Tate was still screaming as he grabbed the man's lank hair and pulled him onto the wickedly sharp blade, and more hot blood frothed from his open mouth, and the man was making a wet, gurgling sound and the colonel, his brown coat made darker with the blood, was grunting as he tried to slice the blade deeper still. He let go, and Wagnon collapsed onto the ground.

Pett began to weep.

'Pick it up,' Tate said.

The rapist backed away.

Tate ran at him. 'Pick it up, you coward!' he bellowed as he thrust the sword into the *fusilier's* belly. Pett let out a pitiful moan that became high-pitched as the cold blade held him there and Tate forced it farther into his body, staring into his blue eyes that were tear-stained, feeling the tip hit stone behind. Blood pumped from Pett's open mouth, and Tate twisted the sword free. The prisoner folded onto the floor, jerked like a landed fish until Tate chopped through his spine and then was still.

Tate held out his sword for *Lieutenant* L'Hanhard to take. 'I want it cleaned, sharpened and oiled and back to me within the hour,' he told the petrified aide.

'Those men—' Le Brun began.

'Those men were nothing,' Tate instantly answered with disdain. 'Some animals always need to be caged,' he added before beckoning Marrock to join him.

'Our cover may be blown,' he said when they were walking away from the property, 'but I want you to take the rest of your men south. There's a road that branches from Fishguard up to those hills.' He pointed to the fields at Garnwnda. 'High plains and craggy hills. I want it secured and watched. If the redcoats come, I want to know about it.'

'Very good, sir.'

'I will leave Captain Didier's and Captain Caillot's men guarding those hills, but I want that road held. I don't trust Le Brun or most of the other officers. I don't trust their nerve,' he said, clarifying what he meant. 'And I don't trust half the men. You've seen what kinds of shit they scraped together to form the regiment. I arrive here, only to find that the scum have already resorted to plundering, looting and raping. What has Le Brun done about that? Nothing! I will issue a statement that if any man is caught raping or molesting the locals, they will be killed on the spot.' He sighed disappointedly. 'And it was going so well,' he said, then laughed cynically.

Marrock didn't ask him about the rules on thieving. 'You did the right thing back there, sir,' he said loyally.

Tate tried to smile, but it came out like a grimace. 'I want the Legion to be remembered for great things, not for rape. We still have orders, and our mission will go ahead with or without that scheming, slimy French bastard's interference.'

Marrock knew Tate was talking about De Marin, who had derided Tate's friendship with Yates and of the American's vendetta towards Sir William Knox. 'What of Major Yates, sir?' the lieutenant asked instead.

Tate looked solemn, then shrugged. 'I have to understand that he might be dead or is a prisoner.'

'If he's alive, won't he talk?'

'I pray not.'

Marrock looked dubious at that response. 'What of the redcoats, sir?'

Tate shook his head scornfully. 'I don't think we need to worry about them. Yates kept me appraised of their garrisons and their strengths over the last few months. We have nothing to worry about. They won't be here for days, and by that time, we'll be somewhere else. However, the Volunteers might indulge us.'

'Is it true about the ships, sir?'

The fleet had left to return to France earlier in the day, leaving the Black Legion to fend for itself. Tate had been informed, and he had informed the senior officers rather than lie to them. 'Marooned or not, we have a job to do. We make our own destiny.'

'Very good, sir.' Marrock saluted and was turning to leave when Tate gripped his forearm.

'Guard that road, but don't pursue any redcoats. I want you and your men to maintain the high ground.'

'Yes, sir.'

'But if you have a chance to kill any redcoats, then don't hesitate.'

Marrock grinned. 'I won't, sir.'

Tate watched him leave, then stood beside an oak tree, where its roots curled up like steps beside its ancient trunk. He climbed up as far as he could and gazed across the valley to where wind stirred the tall grasses and the rustling sounded like waves crashing on the shore.

*

Mullone watched from the crinkled high ground. There was no sign of the French up in the tors opposite, but as Nisbett had said earlier, he felt them close too. What were they going to do now? They had lost the fort and withdrawn. What options were left? What was their mission? Mullone had assayed the scraps of paper that Yates had forgotten to dispose of. They didn't provide much information, mostly directed at the area. There were some letters sent from Tate, written five years ago and one dated last September, but they were of polite conversation between friends. Mullone could see nothing coded in them, but he kept them all anyway.

He checked the time. It was nearly twelve o' clock. He could sense that the Scouts were getting restless, but Nisbett was doing a good job by keeping them alert. The sound of a horse thundering behind made Mullone step away from the summit. It was Lieutenant Nash.

'He's advancing the Newport Division up the Trefwrgi road, Major!' Nash was appalled.

'Where's that?'

Nash pointed to the banked road going north. 'There, sir.'

'Has he received orders?'

'No, sir. He said he was bored.'

Mullone reeled. 'Bored?'

Nisbett sauntered over.

'Colonel Knox has decided, without orders,' Mullone told him, 'to march the Newport Volunteers up the road,' he craned to see, 'I'd guess towards Llanwnda, in the hope of putting an end to his boredom.'

The old captain winced and sucked in his teeth. 'That's a bugger of a road. Narrow and high-hedged. Difficult to manoeuvre.'

87

'I can imagine,' Mullone agreed, having experienced the type of pathway yesterday. 'The French have had plenty of time to make ambush points. What he's doing is reckless.'

'A charnel house,' Nisbett commented.

'What do we do, sir?' Nash asked. 'He's asked me to give orders for the Scouts to provide a screen.'

Nisbett and Mullone exchanged a look.

Mullone could see that the Volunteers were moving across the wider bridge flanking the woods, with the two Colours of the regiment unfurled in the front files. The standards were carried by ensigns, the lowest ranking officer. The Regimental Colour was of a red St George's cross on a white field, with the wreathed regimental title in the centre and surmounted by the feathered badge of the Prince of Wales. A second ensign carried the King's Colour, which was the flag of Great Britain, again with the wreathed regimental title in the centre.

What should have brought a touch of patriotism at the sight, vexed Mullone instead. 'Damn the man!' He strode to untie his horse, put a boot in the stirrups and hoisted himself up into the saddle.

'Your Colonel would lose his arse if it was loose,' Nisbett said to Nash. 'Carelessness can cost lives.'

'I would stay put, Captain. I'll sort this out.' Mullone kicked the beast forward with a stab of his heels to its flanks and rode off down towards the impatient colonel.

Knox saw his approach but pretended that he hadn't. 'Major Mullone,' he said wearily.

'Order your men back!' Mullone told him. 'You are disobeying a direct order!'

'Who is this man?' said a voice beside the colonel.

Mullone saw that it was an officer wearing an expensively tailored coat with gold lace and buttons. His belts and epaulettes gleamed, his buckles and gorget dazzled, and yet Mullone knew this man had never fought in a battle before.

'This is Major Bowen of the Newport Volunteers,' Knox said.

Bowen glared at Mullone with pale, unfriendly eyes that seemed lost in a large, fleshy face. 'Colonel Knox tells me your some sort of government man? Chasing shadows and the like. Not real soldiering is it?'

Mullone gave the major a look that would have killed. 'Tell me what is?'

Bowen was not impressed either. 'Be gone with you, sir. Leave the fighting to Welshmen. We don't need foreigners to fight our battles.'

'You needed one in the fort,' Mullone retorted. 'Where were you?'

Bowen's lips trembled as he fought to control his anger, yet he had nothing to contradict that statement. 'You are not part of the regiment!' he said, a dribble of spit falling from his mouth. 'We don't take orders from the likes of you! Government man!'

Mullone almost bowed with the pressure of that insult. He knew these men were fiercely loyal to one another, coming from the close-knit settlements, and probably viewed his presence with irritation and suspicion. To them, he was just some interfering outsider, and he really did not have any authority over the Volunteers. He had been surprised by the Welsh obeying him during the blood-drenched tussle but had quickly realised that no one else was there to lead them. And that was what they had craved. Leadership. But out here, the men of Newport had their officers with them, and Mullone was a fly in the ointment.

'The Frogs may have landed, but we must defend the king's land from the king's enemies!' Knox said loud enough for the men to hear. They cheered him, leaving him looking smug.

'You are defying orders, Colonel,' Mullone said. 'What will happen if Lord Cawdor is informed?'

Knox looked defiant. 'I should trust that his lordship welcomes drive, spirit and tenacity. *Acta non verba*.' He gave Mullone a cold, flat smile. 'Please do reaffirm to Captain Nisbett that I require the Scouts to move ahead of this column. I want them now, and if he has any objections, tell him he can be replaced.'

Which was a truly stupid thing to say, Mullone thought. Nisbett had more experience of light infantry tactics than anyone here. Nevertheless, Mullone decided to leave before he too said something foolish. He spurred away with the sound of the major guffawing behind.

He would ride back to Nisbett, and Knox would get his way.

*

Lieutenant Marrock shifted his brown gaze along the steep banks and to the road below. A fox had been seen, weaving through the winter-thin hedgerows, but otherwise, for the last hour, the road was empty. He hoped the redcoats would come. He wanted revenge for the embarrassment of being kicked in the throat yesterday, an act which had left him half-choking, and his desires of proving himself had been slighted by the attack. Marrock hoped he would meet that officer again. The cool-headed defiance, the skill in which a handful of the grenadiers were slaughtered in that narrow killing-space galled him deeply. By the time De Marin had brought the rest of the men up, the enemy officer had gone and escaped.

Marrock was from Kildare and had joined the growing bands of Irishmen that wanted British rule in Ireland to cease. He had been brought up to hate the English and didn't care that the redcoats were Welsh. A man wearing a red coat was an enemy through and through. And any redcoat, he vowed, was a dead man.

He commanded forty veterans from the Legion, hidden on the reverse slope of the road's embankments, where they crouched. The muskets were loaded; the black powder, wadding and leaden balls were rammed down the barrels; the locks were primed and the pans open.

They were ready for any redcoats to come.

*

Mullone went with Nisbett and the Scouts to join the two marching companies of the Newport Division. There were groups of onlookers from the villages and settlements and some individuals come to observe. One crossed to the Scouts, and Mullone was about to order the person away when he stopped to stare at him.

'What are you doing here?' he bellowed from horseback. 'Did you allow him to come along?' Mullone turned furiously on Nisbett.

'No, Major,' the old captain lied.

90

Mullone looked back at the figure. 'Go home!'

'It's my land we're fighting for, Major,' came the response as Cadoc threaded his way over to the two men. 'News came to the village from farmers who live up on Pen Caer that the bastards have stolen communion plate and silver from the church and plundered homes. People have been attacked and shot at. I, like the folk here, will not stand by and let it happen anymore!' the boy said firmly, hefting a musket taken from a dead enemy, and Mullone suddenly felt humbled by his determination.

'Very well,' Mullone conceded, 'but keep back out of harm's way.'

'I will, sir.'

Mullone was about to tell Cadoc to let the soldiers do their duty when he realised that the boy had already done more than most of the Volunteers marching. He watched him join the men in the skirmish chain, musket primed and loaded. Cadoc looked happy.

Nisbett ordered the Scouts into double-time, and they scrambled through a break in the hedge banks to clamber up through the other guard, the right flank, as the column rumbled on. Nisbett stabbed the end of his stick into the soft ground with each step, then brought it back with a little flourish. Mullone thought him wonderfully self-assured. Two drummers, both not even fourteen, were dressed in the reverse colours, and their white coats, faced-red, were stark against the colours of the land in winter. They had rattled the men on, but upon climbing the road farther, Knox had ordered them to cease. Nisbett was already through, but the leading men in the narrow road prevented Mullone from joining him. Mullone waited, then brought the horse into the knot of officers, two of which were on foot.

'I'm not taking the men farther than the summit, Major,' Knox told him. 'I just want to see if the Frogs are there, and it will give the men a chance to practise their drill.'

Mullone said nothing and merely looked far ahead where the road revealed itself with every step. It was narrow, barely enough width to allow five men to march in line. 'I would suggest moving the Colours to the rear should the enemy reveal themselves, for they will be like a beacon to them,' he said, and immediately Major Bowen grunted with derision.

'I will order no such thing, Mullone,' Knox said harshly. 'The regiment is proud of its Colours. I want my men to see them in their splendorous glory. The wind stirs the silk, like being Welsh stirs the . . .' Knox pursed his lips as he considered what word to use.

'Blood?' Bowen suggested.

'Yes!' Knox exclaimed. 'Blood, indeed, Major Bowen. Stirs the blood!'

There was a sudden warning before a musket shot fractured the afternoon air. A man gasped, and Mullone tried to see where the noise had come from. A few of the Volunteers halted, only to be pushed back into line by the NCOs. Then there was another musket shot, another, and suddenly a voice shouted and a crash erupted from the banks to the right that plucked redcoats from their feet.

'What's going on?' Knox exclaimed, unable to fathom the dilemma he was now in.

'You've walked into a bloody ambush, Colonel!' Mullone yelled. 'Get your men back!' Knox seemed unable to respond. 'Now!'

Muskets from the Scouts flared above the banks, but they were sporadic, and there were more ambushers. A man screamed and half-fell over the bank's lip, blood dripping from his open mouth. Volunteers were retreating back along the road, but it was chaos. A knot of redcoats at the front were stubbornly holding their ground and aimed their muskets up at the hedges. They pulled triggers, but their volley was wasted because the French crouched back and the flail of leaden balls thrashed the bushes above. Redcoats were falling, tripping and scrabbling to get away.

'Get back!' Mullone ordered, for there was now no point in controlling these raw soldiers to make a slow withdrawal. He had to save lives, not throw them away. There had been a large-bellied oak about two hundred yards back, a good place to reform. 'Get back to the oak! All of you, form at the oak!'

The two ensigns holding the Colours were unable to move because the officers' horses were blocking the path. Mullone yanked Knox's arm. 'Go back, you fool!' he shouted.

Then there was a crescendo of fierce shouts, and Mullone whirled to see twenty or more of the enemy straggling down the powder-fogged banks. He couldn't see Nisbett, or Cadoc for that matter, and it worried him. 'Retreat!' Mullone screamed at the redcoats, but it was too late. Led by an officer, the Frenchmen butchered the Welshmen, then turned to the Colours. Mullone knew they were the enemy's prize, but men were still flooding past him, and Major Bowen seemed helpless to control his horse. Mullone unsheathed his sword and, with the flat side, slapped Bowen's horse on the rump. The startled beast hurtled out of the way. The major, cocked hat now trampled on the ground, shrieked as the beast bolted clear. 'Get back!' Mullone shouted again, but the ensigns either couldn't hear him or were stupefied with fear.

'Stay!' Knox was shouting. 'Stay, you cowards!'

'Back!' Mullone yelled.

Then a musket flamed above, and his horse, struck in the head, collapsed with a grunt onto its knees. Blood fountained from the wound; the force of the shot had driven the mare's right eyeball from the socket. Mullone managed to slide off in time but stumbled against the far bank, sword falling from his hand.

The French officer, young and tall, screamed at the ensigns; his boots thumped on the stony ground. His face was twisted into a mask of horror as he ran, sword-arm swept back. Then he saw Mullone, and the scream turned into a long drawn-out snarl. A redcoat sergeant saw him and brought his musket up, but a bullet fired from above shattered his skull.

'I'll save the Colours, Colonel Knox!' An officer ran past the ensigns to meet the enemy with his own blade. It was Samuel Nash.

Marrock heard the name and saw that there were still three of the four horsemen trapped in the fleeing mass. 'Kill the officers!' he ordered his men. If he could report to Tate that he had slain Sir William's son, then he knew he would be duly promoted.

The Welshman lunged, but Marrock knew the attack was coming, dodged aside and ran his blade hard and up into his body. Nash gasped and his knees buckled. Marrock then gave the blade a savage twist to free, it before running on.

'No!' Mullone yelled as he watched Nash fold.

Yates's horse, eyes wide and yellow teeth bared, kicked and jerked as her heart pumped for the last time. She had rolled backwards due to the gradient of the road, and Mullone's sword was now trapped under her body. Mullone recognised the heavily freckled officer and hauled desperately to free the blade, pulling a length free, but the enemy leapt onto the horse and slashed down with his sword.

'Remember me, you bastard!' Marrock roared.

Mullone drew back as the steel whipped through the air, but there was no room to manoeuvre, and his back slammed into the bank as the sword sliced down own his helmet with an almighty clang. The force jolted his head painfully forwards, leaving a jagged scratch on the brass and dent on the peak.

'Die, you fucking English bastard!' Marrock spat as he brought his sword back to thrust into Mullone's unprotected chest.

'I'm Irish!' Mullone screamed, as he tugged his sword free and sliced it hard, lightning-fast across Marrock's knees. The blade bit through flesh and into bone, and the young Irishman gave a high-pitched shriek before toppling backwards.

'Fire!' a man commanded, and a roar of muskets exploded overheard and into the advancing French.

'The Colours!' Mullone shouted as he got to his feet. 'Protect the bloody Colours!'

The acrid powder smoke hung between the verges and mingled with the metallic-stench of blood. A Welshman crawled back along the road, leaving a trickle of bright blood on the stones.

Another ripple of musket-fire slew three of the closest browncoats. A Frenchman charged at the standards as both ensigns were clumsily backing away, but a musket fired, and the man was snatched backwards, leaving behind a haze of crimson in the air. The rest baulked, having seen their officer fall.

Marrock groaned and shuddered from the agony but still held onto his sword. Mullone stood over him. There was nothing but abhorrence in the young Irishman's eyes. Marrock spat at him and cursed him. He brought his sword up to stab Mullone in the groin, but the attack was feeble, and Mullone knocked the blade away.

'Do it!' Marrock snarled. 'I don't care if you're Irish or not! You're a fucking traitor to your kin!'

Mullone watched him silently. An Irishman about to kill another. There was something shameful in that. The growing troubles in

Ireland were smouldering like the sparks of a great fire to come, infecting the young and old with hatred, like a disease, and that worried Mullone.

Everything seemed to slow down. He was aware of the stabs of flame from the muskets that flickered through the powder haze. Aware of the glowing wadding that drifted in the breeze. He was aware of the splash and drip of blood and the moaning of the wounded.

'Do it, you coward!' Marrock screamed, taking Mullone out of his reverie. '*Erin go Bragh*! Death to the king's men!'

Mullone killed the lieutenant quickly. The sword blade went under his pale chin, up through the back of his mouth and into his brain.

A bullet fluttered past Mullone's ear, and another skittered through branches. He was aware of shouting and the splintering sound of musket-fire, but he was staring at Marrock's dead eyes, fixated by the light that seemed to go out, like a soul departing.

'Major!' a voice was shouting. 'Major!'

Mullone turned to see Nisbett, musket in hand, waving him back. Cadoc was next to him, busily loading his firearm. The road was filled with redcoats, a solid red line formed and made ready by the old veteran. Knox and the other officers had gone. Mullone watched the Colours flutter with the breeze. They had been saved from capture, and Mullone felt his temper bubbling at the one man who had caused this catastrophe.

The Newport Volunteers had reformed by the oak. The French, as far as he could tell, had pulled back beyond the rise, taking their wounded. Mullone, as the highest-ranking officer present, made sure every redcoat casualty was collected. Farms were scavenged for horses and carts, and the dead and wounded were taken away from the road that was marbled with blood. Mullone watched as Nash was unceremoniously hauled up by two privates.

'Steady with him,' Mullone told them. 'The lieutenant was a kind and brave man.' Nash, it had come to light, had given up his horse to allow a wounded private a chance at life.

The two men gently lifted him up onto the straw-filled cart, and Mullone walked over and closed his lifeless eyes. He patted his breast and then as he was the last of the Volunteers, the driver jerked the reins and the cart surged forward.

'The man's gone,' Nisbett said of Knox, 'the bloody man's gone.'

'Any idea where?'

'Aye, towards Haverfordwest,' Nisbett said gravely. 'Along with the other blockheads.' His contempt was naked and pure.

Mullone took his hand and shook it. 'You did well, Captain. You saved the regiment from destruction.'

Nisbett, despite his rancour, was pleased with the praise. 'There's life in this old dog yet,' he said and then barked his usual laugh. A sergeant ran up to him to report something.

Mullone turned to Cadoc, whose face was black with gritty powder. He took the boy's hand. 'And you, Mister Cadoc, have proved again that you have skills with a firearm. I am most impressed. If you would like to serve your country by enlisting, then I shall have a word with Lord Cawdor when I see him. I will tell him of your skills. I'm also sure Captain Nisbett will recommend you.'

Cadoc grinned. 'Thank you, Major. Will I have to serve under a man like the colonel? He's got his brains in his ballocks.'

Mullone laughed. 'The army has an endless supply of idiots,' he said, 'but there are some excellent ones. Men like Captain Nisbett.'

Cadoc took off his hat and scratched his mop of black hair. 'I've decided that it's better to fight than to fish for the rest of my life.' He smiled, then turned serious. 'I was brought up to hate the English.' He shrugged. 'Well, anyone who wasn't Welsh, to be honest. There's a village called Nevern; it's famous because in the church grounds there is an ancient yew tree that bleeds. It is said that it bleeds in sympathy for Jesus Christ, but my father says it won't stop bleeding until the Welsh break free of English rule. He is wrong, of course. I've come to understand who the real enemies are.'

Mullone thought Cadoc was wonderfully shrewd for someone so young. 'Very true, young Arthur. And now the French have stirred the Red Dragon of Wales from its slumber, and more fool them. They've a tempest on their hands, and one they can't hope to win.'

Nisbett cast a look up at the peaks behind them. 'Shall I order our men back to the ridge beyond the marsh?'

Mullone looked at them. 'Yes, I suppose so.'

Nisbett issued the order and the sergeant turned smartly away.

'Lucky buggers are probably going back to the farms to their drink.' Cadoc hawked a wad of spittle into the nearest hedge.

'Drink?' Mullone asked.

'Aye, if they've taken Mortimer's farm and Brystgarn, then more than likely they will have found the wine.'

Nisbett grunted with agreement.

'Wine?' Mullone was struck with a thought. 'Mortimer's farm, are you talking about John Mortimer?'

'The same,' Cadoc returned.

Mullone remembered that the farmer had mentioned a wreck of a Portuguese vessel and wine that had been brought ashore.

'John Mortimer was the first there,' Nisbett explained. 'He was the one that told us of the wreckage. Kegs of port, brandy and wine. Thousands of bottles too.'

'If the Frogs haven't found Mortimer's wine, then we may have found a way to stop this raid once and for all,' Mullone told them, and for the first time that day, he smiled.

Mullone and Cadoc went west. They were on foot and skirted the roads and the curling crags of Garnwnda, ever conscious of possible French positions. They found a hollow half-hidden by a fallen beech tree and decided to stay there until it was dark. Mullone looked east with his telescope before settling down in the sheltered hole. He could see Mortimer's farm, the crisscross of hedges, open fields and shadowy woods. He panned left to right. Grey smoke drifted from the camp fires. Browncoats were camped on the reverse side of the heights and in those fields. There were figures at the farm, although it was too far to see inside the buildings. The men were black figures against the firelight that pitted the encampment. Mullone could see picquets flung out on high ground to guard the invasion force from attack, although none looked their way to the west.

But the farm was not Mullone's destination, nor did he want to slink through enemy lines. There was another stone chamber just to the north, like the one he had hid in, only this one, Cadoc assured him, contained Mortimer's hidden trove of wine and spirits.

'You certain this will work?' Cadoc asked.

'Aye, as certain as there is breath and death in life,' Mullone said. 'Soldiers are ever enticed to drink. For some, it's the only reason they joined up.'

They waited until night was long in the tooth. Cadoc went first, crouching, and followed a weaving trail to the ancient burial stones. They went as quiet as ghosts, like two shadows in a dark world. Mullone was nervous of failure but tried to reassure himself that the plan would work. It had to. A muscle twitched in his left thigh, and he rubbed it to make it stop.

The ground became thick with heather and offered no protection. Mullone's eyes watched for enemies. Cadoc warned him they were approaching a brook, and a bird suddenly flapped and squawked in alarm, its wings beating the wind frantically, but that was the only scare.

'Here!' Cadoc said, after splashing through the water, and Mullone stopped.

The stark mouth of the chamber loomed a few paces ahead. Cadoc went first and, upon reaching the entrance, took off his hat and wrapped it around a stick. He asked Mullone to hold it, and without any charge in the musket, he hauled back the hammer and pulled the trigger. The flint snapped forward, shooting sparks over the wool. Nothing happened. Cadoc tried it again, and by the fifth time, a spark caught and flared swift and bright. The hat, Mullone thought, might have been used by Cadoc to wipe oily or greasy hands.

The torch flickered, and the cold stone was suddenly bathed in soft light, accentuating the stark lines of the limestone.

'We don't have much time, Major,' Cadoc said, sinking the brand into the soft ground. 'The bottles and barrels are in both rooms.'

As so Mullone and Cadoc went to work. Mullone whistled softly at the stores, reckoning there must have been over five hundred bottles of wine and fifty or more kegs and hogsheads of port and brandy. They rolled out a dozen of the kegs and handfuls of the bottles in a trail as far to the farm and enemy lines as possible without being seen. There Cadoc planted brandy and gunpowder-soaked branches of gorse bushes.

When they finished, Mullone was sweating. He pulled a stopper free from a bottle of port and shared a drink with the boy.

'The last thing they'll want to do is face battle in the grey of dawn,' Mullone said.

'Old Mortimer is going to be furious when he finds out what we've done,' Cadoc muttered, then laughed at their mischief.

'Hopefully, he'll come to understand.'

When they were ready, Cadoc sent sparks over specific bushes, and one by one they burst into flame. Mullone shouted, '*Hé! Je l'ai trouvé le vin et le cognac!*' He repeated it until he heard the murmur of voices from the encampment. There were figures looking their way at the lit-up path. He shouted in French again and waved his arms for the enemy to come. 'That's it, the picquets have spotted us! They'll take the bait for sure! Back!' he told Cadoc under the smoke that covered the sky like a pall.

They doubled back along the blazing track, past the hoard of alcohol and away safe into the obscurity of the night.

The Third Day

Friday, 24th February, 1797

Tate's watch chimed a bitter hour, and he climbed out of the Mortimers' bed, shivered because the fire had gone out in the night, put on his coat and went downstairs. The Mortimers had been relocated to a smaller room, under guard. There were a few figures in the kitchen and in the east-facing sitting room, but it was too early for the sun to spread its fiery light, and most men were still asleep. Tate rubbed his bleary eyes. There was coffee, and he was thankful for that. L'Hanhard brought him some cold ham, bread and boiled eggs for breakfast while Faucon tended the fire.

L'Hanhard looked aggrieved.

'What is it?' Tate asked him, his mouth crammed with egg. He noticed that Faucon was also hiding something. 'Well?'

'I think you'd better finish your breakfast, sir,' L'Hanhard told him.

So Tate hurried and went outside in the monochrome light with his two aides, still holding his cup of steaming coffee. 'Are there more desertions?' Already over a hundred and fifty men absconded since the landing. Where had they gone, Tate was not interested. He was concerned that his force was shrinking and that the enemy would know that before he had a chance to complete his mission.

The Black Legion had no tents, and men had found shelter in the buildings, hollows, hedges and dry ditches. There looked a fair amount of them, but Tate was shown the mass of empty bottles and barrels scattered about the camp. His men were drunk. They were deliriously unconscious in heaps. They were slumped where they had simply dropped. The officers had discovered the calamity and quickly bolstered the picquets with those men unaffected or too far from the orgy of drunkenness, but Tate stared at the mass now snoring, groaning, puking and sleep-drunk. Two hundred? More? He realised the invasion was wholly finished.

'Some cannot be woken, sir,' Faucon murmured.

Tate sucked the cold air into his lungs and peeked to the heavens, where stars were still visible in the inky-black sky. His tongue found a piece of egg lodged between two molars, and he sucked it away. He feigned composure. 'Where did they get the liquor from?'

'From what I can tell, they found the stash in an old chamber, a cave-like structure some way to the west,' L'Hanhard replied. 'Some of the men apparently lit torches to guide the rest of them to it. We think the farmer recovered the drink from a shipwreck. There was a lot of it, and the men . . .'

'And the men pickled themselves,' Tate said levelly, detecting the harsh stink of vomit that wafted across the fields.

'Yes, sir.'

Tate sipped his coffee. 'Well, then, there's nothing more we can do here.' He took another look around and calmly tottered back to the farmhouse; the two aides were quick to follow.

Tate ordered Le Brun to see him, as well as Cramer and Dams, who were the senior adjutants. Writing material, paper and ink was brought along with fresh coffee. In thirty minutes, the men were seated around the big kitchen table, paper and quills ready. They watched Tate circumspectly, wondering what proclamation he was going to issue.

Footsteps sounded in the corridor. It was De Marin.

'Why was I not made aware of this assembly?' he asked querulously.

'You hold no military rank here,' Tate told him bluntly.

De Marin watched him impassively. 'My rank exceeds military burdens. You know full well—'

Tate slammed his fist onto the table. 'You have no rank, sir!' he snarled. 'Hoche gave me overall command of the landing. I am the commanding officer of the Legion. Your position here is frankly unexplained!'

That outburst brought an uncomfortable stillness to the room. Le Brun drummed his fingers on the table, cleared his throat, but as eyes turned to him, he said nothing.

'My inclusion with this landing has been approved by people far above Hoche,' De Marin broadcasted.

'Your inclusion has no bearing here at all,' Tate responded as if the agent's remark was not very important.

De Marin walked slowly and purposefully towards the empty far end of the table. 'If it concerns our mission, then it does.' He glanced quickly at the adjutants, poised to recite something. 'What are you doing?'

Tate was tempted to order De Marin to be escorted from the room but realised what he was about to say would needle him, so he bit his tongue. 'I'm going to offer our terms.'

De Marin's eyes widened with incredulity. 'You're surrendering?'

'I'm saving the lives of my men.'

'Surrendering,' De Marin repeated.

'Saving lives,' Tate said forcefully. 'A good general knows when he has been beaten.'

'Even without a fight?' the agent said in a tone that conveyed Tate was a coward.

'Lieutenant Marrock was killed yesterday,' Tate said. 'He followed orders and died doing his duty.'

'That's what soldiers do,' De Marin said pointedly. 'You must fight on.'

'Most men of the Legion are thieves, murderers and deserters,' Tate said. 'Some are soldiers. Marrock was a soldier.' He looked at De Marin as though he was abhorred by his presence. 'You're nothing but a damned clerk of the Directory, a lowly hound sent to do its master's will. Do not presume to give yourself a title here. And do not presume to tell me what to do.' He leaned closer to the edge of the table. 'This incursion is still under my command, so you will obey me, and you will listen.'

De Marin watched silently for a moment, then sat down and waited eagerly for what Tate had to say.

'I want this written down,' Tate said to the adjutants. *'Sir, the circumstances under which the body of troops under my command were landed at this place render it pointless.'* He paused and rubbed his stubbly chin, the dimple a dark slit. 'Disregard pointless. Use unnecessary. Let me repeat, *'render it unnecessary to attempt any military operations, as they would tend only the bloodshed and pillage.'* Tate replayed the last sentence in his head and was happy with it. The quills scratched furiously on the parchment, then stopped as Cramer and Dams caught up. *'The officers of the whole corps have, therefore, intimated their desire of entering into a negotiation upon principles of humanity for a surrender.'*

The adjutants looked up from their messages at each other. Le Brun was nodding fervently with agreement, L'Hanhard and Faucon looked disenchanted, while De Marin simply scowled.

Tate understood the mood now in the room. 'Believe me, gentlemen, this is for the best. Now the final paragraph.' He paused again. *'If you are influenced by similar considerations, you may signify the same to the bearer, and in the meantime, hostilities shall cease. Health and respect, Tate, Chef de Brigade.'* He pursed his lips and nodded to himself. 'Add the date, and I will sign it.' When the terms were completed, he reread them and grunted with approval. Tate took an offered quill and made his mark on both copies. 'I want you two,' he said, looking at Cramer and Faucon, 'at first light to ride to the British lines and offer these terms. I would imagine they will be very surprised to see you. If they wish to come here to offer their stipulations, then I will allow that, of course. I would imagine the pompous British would have their own. The British like making rules as much as they like making taxes,' he said with a chuckle.

But no one else was in the mood for levity.

For the short-lived invasion was over, and they would likely all be prisoners of war.

*

John Campbell of Stackpole Court, 1st Baron Cawdor, received the French terms at a large house belonging to a family called Meyler, which his quartermaster had commandeered as their headquarters.

The doors were flanked with smartly dressed redcoats. The two French officers bringing the conditions had been politely welcomed, offered a drink, which they respectfully refused, and were allowed to leave. Cawdor confirmed that he would send two officers with his reply at ten o' clock.

The drawing room was now crowded with officers seated and standing around two tables of polished walnut joined together and covered with a large map. It was a dark room, despite east-facing windows letting in dull light, and more candles were requisitioned in order for the men to clearly see the chart.

One of the officers tapped a finger a little way to the east of Mortimer's Farm. 'That is where we found the plunder taken from a Portuguese wreck,' Mullone told the gathering. 'I'm informed the headlands here are tricky to manoeuvre and are very dangerous. Even for experienced seafarers, lord. As I have said, there were hundreds of bottles and great hogsheads of spirits stored in that chamber.'

'The damned Frogs had a jolly good time, I'll wager,' voiced a captain called William Lloyd Davies. He had served with the 38th Foot during the War of Independence and seen heavy action at Bunker Hill. Like Nisbett, Davies was on half-pay and had volunteered his services to Cawdor at Haverfordwest, becoming his aide-de-camp. He had a hooked nose, and wore his old uniform with pride despite it being very frayed and discoloured.

'I thought that was an inspired plan, Major,' Colonel John Colby proclaimed. 'Inspired indeed.'

That was greeted with a loud chorus of praise, at which Mullone reddened. Colonel Knox was seated at the back of the room, and glared indignantly at the meeting.

'It was lucky that John Mortimer kept so much,' Mullone said.

'Well done, Mullone,' Lord Cawdor replied. He was forty-three, slim built, with sharp features. He wore his uniform of the Pembroke Yeomanry Cavalry, a short dark-blue dolman jacket with buff facings, silver lace and white breeches. 'I should imagine that a great deal of the French have sore heads and sour bellies come this dawn.'

'*Lead us not into temptation, but deliver us from evil*,' Davies quoted the scripture in his light and feathery voice.

'Exactly,' Cawdor said, delighted with the citation.

'Twenty-three of the enemy were brought in as prisoners by locals this morning,' Colby said. 'Some had their wrists bound behind their backs with coarse twine. Frightening savages, apparently. All reeking of drink.'

'But is it enough for us to outnumber them with our sobriety alone?' Captain Stephen Longcroft of the Royal Navy asked. He was a tall, grave-looking man with curls of black hair like swirling smoke cascading down the sides of his face.

Cawdor turned to Davies. 'What are the enemy numbers, Captain?'

'Reports say between twelve hundred and fifteen hundred, sir.'

Cawdor gazed up at the low ceiling in thought. 'I wonder how many we can discount now?'

'I'm not sure, sir.'

Cawdor felt his newly shaven jaw. 'Ours?'

Davies had taken off his spectacles, rubbed a lens quickly with a handkerchief and then hastily put them back on. 'Six hundred and five men, sir.'

There was a moment of calm as the men collectively considered the implications of battle. A candle in one of the pewter sticks popped nosily.

'Can we include the armed mob, sir?' posed a surly officer of the Cardiganshire Militia.

Cawdor linked his fingers together to make a steeple, on which he rested his smooth chin. 'No, we cannot,' he asserted mildly.

'They number five hundred or more, by my reckoning,' the officer persisted. 'They could prove useful with their pikes, axes and pitchforks.'

'No.'

'We should attack now that the enemy are completely indisposed,' a yeomanry officer suggested.

'We don't really know the true extent of the drunkenness,' Davies said. 'A great deal might be as drunk as David's sow, but we are still outnumbered.'

'Our men are stout of heart,' chirped another officer.

'That is not the issue,' Davies retorted.

'We need the mob,' the militia officer insisted.

Cawdor shook his head fiercely. 'I will not consider the question of drafting in the locals again. Please move on. Now what do we know of this Colonel Tate?'

'What will that prove?' Knox ridiculed.

Cawdor shot him a lingering glare. The two men had almost come to blows yesterday afternoon when Knox had encountered Cawdor's advance force of the Pembroke Yeomanry on the road to Haverfordwest. When the peer had questioned what Knox was doing there, the young colonel produced his commission and tried to pull rank. Cawdor politely told him that Lord Milford had given him overall command of the military forces in the area and that Knox should put himself under his authority. He did so, but with an outcry that made Cawdor accuse Knox of cowardice in the face of the enemy having learned of the ambush. The young colonel fell silent yet remained aggrieved.

'I'm enquiring because I want to know what sort of man I'm facing,' Cawdor pronounced tetchily. 'I want to know if his terms are to be trusted. After his guise tricked your men, who knows what he's capable of.'

Knox growled. 'My major was in league with the devils. I was not to know their schemes!'

'I have a doubt that you know little of anything,' Cawdor muttered.

Knox visibly bristled. 'Understanding the American makes not one whit of difference.'

'I believe him to be an experienced soldier,' Mullone said quickly, breaking up any chance of an argument. 'He fought during the last war. He's a skilled commander, and I suspect that's why he was chosen to lead the Black Legion.'

'Sounds like some damned mercenary,' Major Dudley Ackland of the Pembroke Yeomanry scoffed.

'He's proven himself and given the rank of *chef-de-brigade*,' Mullone said, 'so no, not a mercenary. A small part of the French are good solid troops, but I can't speak for the rest of them.' He remembered the Irish officer, but decided that was, for now, unimportant. 'We've heard the stories of looting, destruction and marauding.'

'They used St Gwyndaf's Church as a latrine,' Major Bowen commented.

Cawdor hissed in utter revulsion. 'Desecrating God's house in such a way.'

'The French are nothing but filthy animals with no morals,' Ackland uttered.

Mullone waited for the rumble of conformity to subside. 'We know their intent was to cause panic and unrest,' he said. 'Possibly to move north. And they failed.'

'The failed indeed,' Colby said, placing his fists on the table. 'Their nerve has gone. It's over for them.'

'Agreed,' Davies put in, the candlelight reflected in his glasses.

'But what if Tate changes his mind?' Cawdor put to the room.

Colby shrugged. 'He won't.'

'We don't know that,' Cawdor offered the rebuke gently. 'I want an unconditional submission. I want them to lay down their arms and their equipment and return anything stolen. Then I will be happy to have them escorted to prison. I'll let Lord Milford sort that out. Let them be his problem, not ours. I champion the sentiment that there should be no more bloodshed. I want Tate believing that he has no other option but to accept our terms because we have superior numbers.'

'Which is not true,' Ackland said.

'Exactly,' Cawdor replied, as though anyone not understanding that was a simpleton. 'I need them believing that so there is no question of a total yield.'

'The only way of doing that is by dispersing our force in a way that will convince Tate he's facing an army,' Mullone suggested. 'Perhaps shroud the hills with the locals. It might well add weight.'

'Preposterous,' Knox murmured at the back.

Mullone wanted to hit him. Knox, as far as Mullone could see, had nothing positive to give and was only here, because of his standing as the Volunteers' commanding officer.

'Might work,' Davies commented hesitantly.

Cawdor eyeballed Mullone. 'You mean like bluffing in a game of three card brag?'

Mullone winced at the slightly basic analogy but bobbed his head. 'Yes, sir. It's unlikely that he knows our true numbers.'

Mocking wittering erupted from the back of the room, but Cawdor seemed to like the idea.

'I think that's a splendid idea, sir,' Davies said, giving the argument some added credence. 'Forgive me for my impertinence, but I think Major Mullone is saying that they will not be used as part of our force, but to bolster the numbers against the enemy.' He gave Mullone a knowing look, who dipped his head with concord. 'Give the impression of size and write that with every hour our force increases. Something to persuade Colonel Tate with.'

Cawdor trusted his opinion greatly and gave it serious consideration. 'Very well,' the lord said, giving a flutter of his hands that might have been construed as conformity. 'I was against such a notion, but if it's done right, no one will get hurt. Very good. See if you can marshal the locals onto the high ground,' he said to Davies. 'Put our men near the French lines, between the inhabitants, to act as a bulwark in case the mob gets nasty.'

'The women and children will likely want to be there, sir,' Davies said.

'Very well. Allow it, but they must be warned to stay back, otherwise I'll have them arrested. That goes for the men too.'

'Yes, sir,' Davies answered. 'I was thinking that if there are any spare caps and uniform coats, we might lend them to the mob, again to bluff our numbers.'

'If you think that will work, then I'm happy to agree to that,' Cawdor said.

There was a commotion outside the room, and a captain wearing the yeomanry uniform opened the door.

'What is it, Owen?' Cawdor asked.

'There is a local Methodist here, sir, who wants to bless the council.'

Knox rolled his eyes.

'There is no time for that now,' Cawdor said cheerfully. 'Tell him God is needed for the French!'

The room spluttered with laughter, and Cawdor drew up his terms, now bolstered with a hand to bluff Tate into an unequivocal surrender.

*

'The British will be here in less than two hours,' Le Brun said to Tate, who had dressed himself in a simple dark-blue coat and matching breeches. A sword hung at his hip, but there was no other insignia to prove that he was an officer.

'The terms will be agreed upon,' Tate replied lightly. 'Just agree to their demands and use Didier's and Caillot's men to guard the troublemakers, if needs be.'

Le Brun gawked at Tate's coat. 'And where are you going?'

Tate ignored the aristocrat's impudence. He strode over to the table he had used to read dispatches and folded a chart into quarters which disappeared into one of his front coat pockets.

Tate heard a derisive sound and whipped around to confront Le Brun, but his deputy had left and De Marin was now present.

'Couldn't you have chosen a plainer coat in which to dazzle the English?' the Frenchman mocked, speaking in excellent English. He himself was now resplendent in a uniform of the French *Légion Irlandaise*, a scarlet coat faced green. His red hair, caught with the morning's blaze of light, seemed to shimmer.

'It's not the coat that makes the man,' Tate replied glibly, then let his eyes wander disdainfully over the red coat. 'I could have you shot, Mister Spy,' he said and brightened up. 'I would imagine a lot of my men would enjoy killing a redcoat, as would I.' He tapped the pommel of his sword with his hand.

De Marin smiled at the threat. 'Bloodshed on the eve of surrender? That's not what the famed Colonel Tate would want to be remembered for.'

'You know nothing about my desires.'

'Sir William Knox,' De Marin said and then smiled at the expression on Tate's face. 'You are dressed not for indulging the English, but to complete the only true mission you have only ever been thinking of. You care not one whit about the success of the

112

Legion. You have only ever cared about retribution.' He paced over to Tate. 'Of course, the Directory knew this from the start.'

'Really?' Tate looked askance.

'You think they didn't know what was being said or orchestrated?' De Marin laughed mirthlessly. 'You had a record that was interesting, yet hardly admirable. You were chosen because you and the Legion are expendable. Why would the Directory send proper troops when scum was easily available? Rabble cannot achieve success, but they can cause fear, and fear is what the prime directive of this mission was. Not to burn cities or stand in line and shoot volleys. Fear is the first and chief weapon of war. Fear amongst the common people. And the farmers, fishermen, salters, cheesemongers and cobblers have been terrorised. Your mission is complete. Your personal vendetta has no bearing on this raid. The job is done. You and the men will be taken as prisoners. It will be humiliating, but you will live and will be paroled. Possibly exchanged, and France will welcome you. You may not ever lead a Legion again. You might not even retain your rank. But you'll be alive. Deviate from that, fulfil your pathetic feud, and you'll hang.' De Marin smiled again. 'But perhaps that might be the best course of action for the great Colonel Tate,' he said, then continued in a bad American accent, 'all the way from Carolina.'

Tate tried not to let the mockery affect him. He opened his mouth but quickly shut it again. 'So what will you do now? The ships have gone.'

'Not all of them.'

'You'll stay to witness the surrender? That's brave of you.'

'I will stay, although my reasons for doing so aren't what you think. I have no wish to see the Legion die, but I suspect to see an old enemy, and I wouldn't miss that for the world.'

Tate frowned but did not ask for an explanation. 'What will you do then? Vanish like a ghost?'

'My departure is no concern of yours,' De Marin uttered. 'By the time your men ground arms, the both of us will have gone our separate ways. Off to a place where destiny calls.' He gave Tate an elegant bow, then straightened and smiled. '*Bon voyage, Chef-de-Brigade.*'

Mullone and Davies were chosen as the two messengers to deliver Cawdor's terms. Mullone was elated to be reunited with *Tintreach* and had stolen a small amount of sugar from the pantry, so that his stallion had licked his cupped hand greedily.

Now the two men cantered up to the French lines where a group of officers met them. The two British officers followed the Frenchmen up towards Mortimer's farmhouse. Mullone saw that the browncoats had been formed into companies, but most were slumped and sat in groups, as though they had already resigned to their fate. There were well over a thousand. Cawdor didn't need to bluff, Mullone thought. The job is done because Tate had not even bothered to conceal men.

Two *sous-lieutenant*s took their horses to the stables, and Mullone and Davies were offered coffee, which they gratefully accepted. They were seated in the kitchen, where officers watched them. Mullone could detect no hostility in their eyes, just disappointment.

A slender man with thick black hair greeted them. He spoke in French. '*Je suis Chef-de-Bataillon Jacques-Phillippe Le Brun, en Commandant de la 1er Bataillon, 2e Légion des Francs,*' he said with a small bow.

Mullone introduced himself and Davies and then stared at the man entering the room. His face instantly hardened.

'*Bonjour, mon ami,*' De Marin said cheerfully.

'Is this the fellow you were talking about?' Davies asked out of the corner of his mouth.

'Aye,' Mullone uttered with disdain. He remembered the shock of seeing him dressed in the coat of the Legion two days ago, but he now wore Irish Legion attire. Mullone shook his head. 'Still wearing a uniform that you aren't entitled to,' he said to De Marin in English.

The agent plucked at the coat theatrically. 'Oh, I joined the brotherhood on Wolf Tone's insistence,' he replied casually. 'He's a charismatic man. He'll go far. He came to see me in Paris last year. Had interviews with Carnot and De La Croix, as I'm sure you know,' he smiled knowingly. 'We were impressed by his sincerity, energy and passion for his cause.'

'He's wanted for treason, so tell him that he'd better be careful where he travels next,' Mullone said.

De Marin's eyebrows rose and he waved his hands histrionically. 'Is that a threat?'

Mullone smiled, though it showed no warmth. 'More than your wee flash in the pan.'

Le Brun looked at each man, then, deciding that the terms needed to discussed rather than trade idle threats, he offered Mullone and Davies a seat.

'Will Colonel Tate not partake of this meeting?' Davies asked.

Le Brun told them that Tate was unwell, and yet Mullone knew they were being lied to. Even De Marin shook his head at the poor deception.

'He has gone,' Le Brun offered with a shrug.

'Where?' Mullone demanded.

Le Brun could offer no explanation and shrugged his shoulders again. 'But I am now in overall command,' he explained, hoping the matter would close. 'I will listen to your terms, and I have the authority to sign them.'

Mullone looked at De Marin, who tilted his head and grinned. 'The colonel has plans, *mon ami*.'

'And what are yours?' Mullone asked. 'You'll never duly surrender, for once they find out who you are, they'll keep you alive for interrogation.'

'You are right. And I always thought we would pass like ships in the night, Major,' De Marin said with a chuckle that showed little amusement.

Mullone scowled impotently, unable to apprehend the man now. Perhaps, he thought, the Royal Navy might, and so allowed that thought to nullify his anger.

Le Brun read Cawdor's terms. He passed it to De Marin who gave the shortest of nods after reading it.

'I trust you realise that you are simply outnumbered and outgunned,' Davies said in French. 'It is folly to continue. I can arrange safe passage for your men to march down to Goodwick

115

sands, the shore directly here.' Davies produced a map and tapped the area with a finger. 'British troops will make sure your men are not savaged by the locals, and believe me, they would relish such an opportunity. Whereupon, your men are requested to pile arms and equipment on the beach. Your officers will receive treatment to their rank.'

Le Brun clicked his fingers, and more coffee was served, but within ten minutes, the Frenchman had signed the declaration and agreed to organise the Legion to leave within the hour.

'Until we meet again, *mon ami*,' De Marin said to Mullone, as he got up from his chair.

'I hope it's soon,' Mullone growled back.

De Marin flourished his adversary a wide, mocking grin.

The two British officers were escorted to their horses, and they trotted out of the camp and down towards the road to Fishguard. Already British troops watched them from the heights.

Mullone slowed his horse. 'I have some business to attend to, Captain.'

Davies looked startled. 'That damned Frog spy?'

'No, he'll have to wait another day,' he said heavily. 'It's something else. I'll be back later to offer my congratulations.'

And so he wheeled *Tintreach* away and galloped south.

*

Tate tipped over another barrel of turpentine, which gushed across the carpeted floor of the ornately decorated room. Cabinets, side tables, bookcases and bureaus of polished walnut, crafted by the likes of William Hallett and Thomas Chippendale, were now dark with the liquid. Volumes and noted books had been pushed and tipped and thrown onto the floor. Shelves had been hammered and broken. A rosewood writing table and a mahogany *bonheur du jour* now lay in a splintered mess. But the destruction did not end there. Mirrors, candelabras, glass and fine china had been smashed in the kitchen, bedrooms and dining room. Paintings and ornaments were slashed and crushed.

116

Tate surveyed the devastation, not with a smile, but a look of fury. He was wet with sweat, his chest panted as though it had been torn apart by musket-fire, his muscles were strained and he felt like weeping. The American climbed the dark wooden stairs. He had a final job to do here. His nostrils wrinkled at the stink of the turpentine that he had procured from an outbuilding. What he needed now was a flame, for this house must burn.

'He's not here, is he?' a voice called from below.

Tate spun round to see a British officer standing in the long antechamber. Tate had not heard the man enter, although his thoughts had been elsewhere, too distracted to notice.

'Who are you?'

'Major Lorn Mullone,' came the reply. 'We've not met before, although I know you.' He walked forward a few steps revealing both men were of the same build, height and of similar age. 'He's not home now, is he? Sir William Knox. He owns this estate as well as another. I say it was good luck for him that he isn't here, and a pity for you because it's over, Colonel William Tate. It's over.' He saw the look of astonishment on the American's face. 'I was the man who took the fort from you. And I prevented your friend Yates from committing suicide.'

'He's alive?' Tate gasped.

'Oh, a little shaken,' Mullone replied, 'but very much alive.'

Tate stared into Mullone's eyes and found he was speaking the truth. 'Not for long though.'

Mullone gave a slight shrug. 'He's a traitor and he deserves a traitor's fate.'

'He told you about me?'

'No, he hadn't been that confessional. I was more interested in your mission. And by that I mean Hoche's goal.'

'So how did you know where to find me?'

Mullone shrugged. 'I pieced it together. While your second, Le Brun, was signing the British terms, I kept asking myself where you might have gone. Yates left a cryptic message. Something about someone who "will never see another sunrise again". I thought to myself, that was odd. Of all the defiant things he could have said, he chose to say that. Was he talking about himself? I wondered. Or was he thinking of an impending battle. I thought hard about that. He left some letters from yourself, which I read. I gleaned a few names from them, but nothing seemed to jump out to me. Then I remembered the name Llanstinan. It's written on my map. I thought it was the name of an area, not being from around here, but Llanstinan Manor, this very building, is one of Sir William's homes, and it reads clear as a bell. In one of your letters, you wrote about your old friend Sir William Knox. He's not really a friend, is he? That's why you weren't there to receive our terms; you had already decided to come here and see him. One last mission to complete. Or had it been that wish from the very start and the invasion was just a means? But the question remains, and forgive me for my discourtesy, what grudge do you have against him?'

Tate went still and sighed. 'My family,' he uttered, drawing out a cigar from his coat pocket. He casually descended the steps and walked into the nearest room; the floor was littered with debris.

Mullone followed him at a careful distance. His nose and throat clogged from the harsh-smelling liquid.

Tate seemed to be searching for something and then pulled up what appeared to be a pistol. Mullone instantly tugged free his sabre, but then he saw that Tate was holding a gentleman's pistol tinder lighter. It was a curious device that only wealthy men could afford. The handle and flintlock mechanism resembled a pistol, but there was no barrel, only a pan that contained a piece of dry tinder. It was used by hauling back the hammer to cock it, the pan cover was left open and when the trigger was pulled, it sent a spark down into the tinder. That could then be applied to light candles. Tate used Sir William's to light the cigar. He puffed away, letting the tobacco smoke curl about him. He turned to Mullone and gave a lopsided grin at the bare steel.

'I knew many Irishmen from the wars,' Tate said. 'Honest as rogues, but damned fine men all the same. Good soldiers.'

'If this is an attempt directed at my loyalty, then please stop,' Mullone told him. 'I know which side I'm on. It's a pity your young Irish officer didn't.'

Tate's eyes opened fractionally. He sucked silently on the cigar for a while. 'Did you kill him?' he said eventually.

'Yes.'

Tate seemed to think about that. 'He was a soldier.'

'He was, and he died for your cause with a blade in his hand.'

'A good way for a warrior to go,' Tate said, spitting out a shred of tobacco leaf. He glanced around the room. 'Sir William would know nothing about that. He's a snivelling English coward. With a strike of his quill, he was responsible for my family's death. I daresay he didn't even leave his room.'

'So that's why you're here,' Mullone muttered. 'How you must have hoped to find him home, and how crushing for you to discover it vacant.' He gazed about the wreckage. 'Expensive items now fit for kindling.'

'It's nothing compared to the cost of life!' Tate suddenly screamed. 'That poxed bastard took everything from me!'

'I know he did and I'm sorry. Come with me,' Mullone said, outstretching a hand. 'Let's leave this grand place fit for pompous idiots and preening peacocks. Come with me, back to Fishguard. If you give me your word you'll not cause trouble, you can keep your sword. Lord Cawdor will want to question you, but he's decent enough. You'll be treated well and with respect. Just come back with me.'

Tate understood the generosity. 'I thank you, Major,' he said kindly, then sighed heavily. 'I appreciate your words, but I can't leave just yet.'

'Why not?' Mullone said, stiffening and realising only too late what was going to happen.

'Fate,' Tate answered.

The cigar hurtled through the air, the end glowing red like a dying star, and it exploded against a pile of tossed books. There was a pause as the embers burst free, twirled in a glittering dance, and then the flames spread, and suddenly Mullone's world was one of bright illumination and fierce heat.

He backed out of the room, hand protecting his face, and that was when Tate slammed into him. Both of them tumbled to the floor. Mullone rolled and reached out for his sword when Tate kicked him in the chest. The American then ran towards the stairs, but Mullone had recovered and brought him down on the steps. Tate swung his arms to hit Mullone in the face, but the Irishman pushed the colonel's head hard against the wood.

'You're coming with me!' Mullone yelled. He grabbed Tate's collar and used all his strength to throw him backwards.

Tate reached out to grab the banister, and Mullone pulled to rip his blue coat. Tate then back swung his right fist, which hit Mullone in the face. He then lashed out with a boot, and the blow struck Mullone in the belly. Tate shoved, and Mullone lost balance and tumbled down the steps, painfully jarring his hands and wrists as he crashed into the hallway.

Smouldering, the fire licked around the walls, leaping and flaring, crackling and flickering like a devouring fiend. It had spread fast, incredibly fast, and plumes of black choking smoke roiled out into the hallway and up to the high ceilings.

Mullone turned, saw a blaze spread along the carpet and rolled as the fire began to spread to the other rooms that had been doused in the flammable liquid. Ash floated in the searing air, like dirty flakes of snow. The intense heat hurt the bare skin of his hands as he shielded his face.

'Tate!' he bellowed, but the American had disappeared upstairs. 'Tate!'

Mullone knew he had to follow him up there. It was risky, but he considered life was all about risk.

He jumped the flames and raced up the stairs. The rooms were as wrecked as the others. Debris and ruination was everywhere. Mullone searched, but each room was deserted. Where was he? Then a great shower of sparks came from one of the rooms to the west of the building making him jump.

'Tate!'

He passed a small room engulfed with red flame and moved on. Then he heard a dull thud and turned back to find the doorway was now blocked with a large bookcase. Inside the hellish room stood a figure.

'Tate!' Mullone called and began to heave at the bookcase, but it seemed to be too heavy to move. The heat was weakening him, searing him. 'Help me move this bloody thing!' He yelled, but Tate remained motionless with a serene look on his long face.

Mullone thought he looked completely dignified.

Droplets of fire spilled from the ceiling. More books twisted and curled to ash. The curtains were like ribbons of hellfire. Smoke wound around the doorway like a serpent.

'Tate! For God's sake!'

'It's too late for me,' Tate told him. Tears of sorrow, or caused by the heat, shone in his pale eyes. 'It's over now.'

'Don't be a bloody martyr! Come with me! I'll help you!'

'My mission was doomed from the start. There is no reason for you to join me. Go, Major.'

'Tell me about De Marin,' Mullone asked. 'What part did he play in this? What do you know of him? You can help me find the bastard. We can help each other.'

'I will now see my family again. Goodbye, Major.'

And then a deafening crash came from above, and smoke and flame erupted from the room, sending Mullone backwards, away from the red-hot fire.

'No!' he bellowed, but he knew the colonel could not be saved. He had chosen his fate.

Mullone staggered away and thumped a fist onto the wall out of frustration.

The floorboards lurched under Mullone's weight. Flames flickered across the carpet and up the staircase; smoke obscured the antechamber. Wood crackled and split. The only way down was to vault the rail as Mullone fancied he could do nothing else to escape this inferno.

He hit the floor with a thud, recovered, glimpsed the encroaching flames with a look of sadness, then ran for the door.

The Black Legion had marched down to Goodwick and laid down their arms and equipment as per their instructions. British drummers and one fifer played 'Men of Harlech' loudly in an attempt to drown out the catcalls and taunts from the locals, who watched from the heights above the beach, where rare choughs nested in holes and crevices.

Mullone arrived back to see the defeated French formed into a long column under a weak and fickle sun, where small waves lapped wearily on the shore. He watched the dark blood-coloured uniforms, some wearing greatcoats, gloves and crude cloaks, shivering under guard. Mullone wondered if that was from trepidation or from the February wind that blew across the sea.

Two British ships were anchored in the harbour, not frigates, but Revenue cutters, brought up from Milford by Captain Longcroft. But there was no need for the vessels now; the French fleet had gone. His eyes traced gulls circling in the rinsed sky.

'They're being sent on to Haverfordwest,' said a genial voice to Mullone's left. It was Captain Davies, Cawdor's aide. 'From there, they will be escorted down to the Hampshire coast and put in transport at Portsmouth.'

'Not the hulks, then?' Mullone enquired without looking at him.

Davies shook his head. 'A motley collection of soldiers, if you ask me. No, it's being arranged for a quick deportation. No one wants to feed them, you see. They're a forlorn lot.'

'What about the officers?'

'Most will be questioned but offered parole. We are missing two. Colonel Tate and a Captain Le Haillan.'

'I'm afraid Le Haillan might possibly be a French agent called De Marin. I doubt you'll find him.'

'I see. And Tate?'

Mullone said nothing. He continued to watch the white gulls skitter in the limpid sky like scraps of parchment tossed to the wind.

Davies rubbed his tired face. 'We've already uncovered a group of the rank and file hiding in one of the old burial chambers. They looked like tramps.'

'Probably looking for more wine,' Mullone remarked wryly.

Davies chortled. 'I suspect you're right, Major. If there's a chance to apprehend any more stragglers, we'll get them. Maybe we'll even strike gold and catch that spy of yours, eh?' He gave Mullone a shrewd smile. He looked at his battered face and offered a hand. 'I have to depart. Paperwork beckons and billet expenses have to be accounted for. Lots of work to be done. Lord Cawdor, as well as many others including myself, are very grateful for your assistance, Major. I want you to know that.'

Mullone shook his hand. 'It was a pleasure to meet you, Captain.'

Davies gave a curt nod, clicked his horse forward, and Mullone watched him disappear down the twisting path towards Fishguard. It was then that he saw a figure walking towards him.

'Are you a Volunteer yet, young Arthur?' he enquired with a grin.

'No,' Cadoc replied, musket slung on a shoulder, 'I've decided to enlist.'

'Have you now? Well, that's good news for King George. He's got a rare man on his side.'

'Thank you, Major,' Cadoc said, flushed with pride. 'Will you be going home soon?'

'Not for a few days. There's a ship that sails to Cork on Tuesday, so I'm told.' He patted *Tintreach*'s face affectionately. 'We'll both be looking forward to going home, won't we, boy?' he said tenderly. The stallion whickered a contented reply. 'You need to have new shoes. And a few days rest. You've earned it and more, boy. I don't know what I would do without you.' Mullone patted again, then looked at Cadoc. 'There'll be plenty of time for the two of us to share some ale and talk.'

'I'd like that very much, Major.'

'Good. And heaven knows I need a drink,' Mullone said, then grinned, feeling his spirits lift.

And then he would go to Ireland. Home, he thought wistfully, a place he couldn't stop thinking of. Troubles were brewing like the beginnings of a storm. A tempest, conceivably like the one here in Wales. And he would be needed there if more dark plots threatened his beloved home.

He stared out across the grey water, over the masts and rigging, where in the breeze, the union flag flew bright above the fort. The French had lost and had surrendered beside the sea. It was over.

HISTORICAL NOTE

I have to admit that with *Tempest*, I took a few liberties, and I do hope you'll forgive me for them. I have always tried, within the constraints of fiction, to stay true to historical fact. For those embellishments and more, I'll explain the reasoning behind any changes.

The brief campaign, and it was very brief, should be regarded as the 'Last Invasion of Great Britain', rather than the combat-sounding 'Battle of Fishguard' because, quite simply, there was no battle. I much prefer the 'Battle *for* Fishguard' as it has a better and more truthful ring to it.

The landed invasion, which started on 22nd February, ended just two days later. It was the plan of Lazare Hoche, who had devised a three-pronged attack on the British Isles in support of Irish Republicans under Wolfe Tone. Two forces were to land as a diversionary effort while the main body would be sent to Ireland. While bad weather halted the first landing (Bantry Bay, December 1796), indiscipline terminated the second intended at Newcastle, and the third, aimed at bombarding Bristol and landing troops. The objective of the third was to start an uprising against the English using the deep-rooted patriotism and nationalist pride in the Celtic regions of Great Britain and march to Chester, Liverpool and Manchester.

The fleet of four ships, under the command of Commodore Jean-Joseph Castagnier, set sail from Brest on 16th February flying Russian Colours. The four French warships were some of the newest and largest in the French fleet: the frigates *La Vengeance* and *La Resistance* (the latter being on her maiden voyage), the corvette *La Constance*, and a smaller lugger called *Le Vautour*.

Rough weather altered their plans, and the fleet could not enter Bristol. On their way through the Channel, the fleet was spotted from Ilfracombe flying British Colours, but changing their plan to Wales, they were spotted off the coast of Pembrokeshire by retired sailor Thomas Williams of Trelythin. He saw the decks crammed with troops and reckoned they were French, not British, and so raised the alarm.

The fleet captured a British trading vessel, the sloop *Britannia*, carrying a cargo of culm bound for Fishguard, whose Captain John Owen bluffed the French of the dangers of trying to land there when it was defended by infantry, cavalry and artillery emplaced at Fishguard Fort.

The invasion force consisted of nearly fifteen hundred soldiers from the *La Legion Noire* (The Black Legion) under the command of American Colonel William Tate. Tate was of Irish decent and did have a hatred towards the British after his parents were butchered by pro-British Native Americans during conflicts between the French, Spanish and Dutch, before the American War of Independence. But he was in no way connected to Sir William Knox and the revenge storyline in *Tempest* is a fabrication. Tate served with the South Carolina Continental Artillery, and after the war became embroiled in a scandal involving the embezzlement of public funds. He was then implicated with a raid in Florida against British possessions and fled to France before capture. He is often, incorrectly, described as an old man around seventy, when in fact he was a veteran of the colonial wars, aged forty-four at the time of the invasion.

The French soldiers were indeed a mixed bag, and this would have ramifications and cause Tate to surrender on the 24th. He had at his disposal four hundred revolutionary soldiers that had not been needed for Bonaparte's Italian campaign. There were a further two hundred Breton rebels pressed into service nicknamed *chouans* a moniker taken from Jean Chouan, a Breton who had led a major revolt against the French Revolution. The remaining eight hundred were indeed the worst scum imaginable. Mostly deserters and convicts, many embarked Brest on 16th February in chains and were still in chains when they surrendered.

The Black Legion had been issued with British red coats that had been supplied by the government to rebels fighting in the Vendée before being acquired and coloured with poor quality black dye. The result left the coats a brown or dark rust colour, hence giving *La Seconde Légion des Francs* the soubriquet. Facings were described as sky-blue and were probably the original colour. The headgear were described as old cavalry caps, leather with horsehair manes, while other reports say the French wore bicorne hats.

The fleet anchored around four o'clock in the afternoon off Carregwastad Point, Pembrokeshire, on the 22nd. Perhaps they chose this spot because Captain Owen had warned them about entering Fishguard's harbour. A failed attempt to enter the harbour is mentioned in various accounts, but this does not seem to have appeared in print before 1892, and was taken from a children's story. I decided to have Tate meet Yates on the shore to reveal more of their friendship and to allow the browncoats to sneak into the story. This was really a nod to the Germans playing free Polish troops in the novel *The Eagle Has Landed* by Jack Higgins, a favourite of mine.

By two the next morning, seventeen boatloads of soldiers, forty-seven barrels of powder, fifty tons of cartridges and grenades and two thousand firearms had been brought ashore. This was indeed a magnificent feat despite losing one boat containing stores. A company of grenadiers under Irishman, *Lieutenant* Barry St Leger, whom Marrock is loosely based on, rushed a mile inland and took over Trehowel Farm, a substantial building which did become Tate's headquarters.

The French moved a further two miles inland and occupied two strong defensive positions at Garnwnda and Carngelli, high rocky outcrops that give an unobstructed view of the surrounding countryside. Tate had every reason, at this time, to be confident in the success of the invasion.

With the loss of the American colonies in 1783, the last Under-Secretary of State, Sir William Knox, decided in 1784 to purchase estates in Pembrokeshire, and his mansion at Llanstinan was only four miles from Fishguard. When the government called for Volunteers in the war against the French, Knox subsequently raised the Fishguard and Newport Volunteer Infantry in 1794, one of the earliest in the kingdom. His son, Thomas Knox, was appointed lieutenant-colonel. At the time of the French landing, Knox was twenty-eight years old, had purchased the rank and had no combat experience. He was attending a social function at Tregwynt Mansion when news of a suspected enemy landing was brought to him. Initially, he gave it little credence, but as the seriousness of the situation dawned on him, he immediately instructed his Newport Division to march the seven miles to his headquarters at Fishguard Fort to meet up with the Fishguard Volunteers, bringing him a total of around two hundred and seventy men.

Lieutenant-Colonel John Campbell, Lord Cawdor, was thirty miles away at Stackpole Court in the far south of the county when he received the news of the invasion. He had been commissioned captain of the Castlemartin Troop of the Pembroke Yeomanry Cavalry, which fortunately was assembled for a funeral on the following day. He immediately mobilised all the troops at his disposal and crossed the Pembroke Ferry with the Pembroke Volunteers and the Cardiganshire Militia. Once across, Cawdor went ahead and met Lord Milford, the Lord Lieutenant of the county, who delegated full authority to him with a brevet rank of lieutenant-colonel.

Most of the credit for gathering about four hundred soldiers and sailors at Haverfordwest was due to the energy of Lieutenant-Colonel John Colby of the Pembrokeshire Militia. Having summoned the troops to Haverfordwest, he had galloped the sixteen miles north to Fishguard to assess Knox's situation. Satisfied that Knox was taking appropriate measures, he returned to Haverfordwest to supervise the force. Captain Stephen Longcroft of the Royal Navy brought in the press gangs and the crews of two Revenue cutters at Milford, totalling about one hundred and fifty sailors. Nine cannons were brought ashore, of which six were placed in Haverfordwest Castle, and the others were transported on hay-carts with the reinforcements, which set off at noon.

Knox had boasted to Colby that he intended to attack the following day if he was not heavily outnumbered. Colby wrote after the invasion that he had suggested to the young colonel that he should place troops on the heights opposite the French to discourage them from moving until reinforcements could be brought up. Knox did indeed send out Scouts under the command of Captain Thomas Nisbett, an experienced veteran of the Colonial Wars who was waiting for passage to Ireland, as a picquet line.

Although many inhabitants were fleeing the area in panic, hundreds of civilians were flocking into the area armed with a variety of crude weaponry.

But as the hours ticked on, the reality must have hit Knox. He faced a dilemma: to wait for reinforcements and defend, or to withdraw towards the troops coming up from the south, which he knew would be moving towards him that afternoon. He issued the orders for a total withdrawal, abandoning the villages of Fishguard and Goodwick and the fort, all of which would have severe implications afterwards. He also gave orders to spike Fishguard Fort's cannons, which the Woolwich gunners refused to carry out.

The fort did have eight serviceable nine-pounders, but there were only three rounds in the magazine. There was no fight for the stronghold and what's in *Tempest* is pure invention.

Knox and his Volunteers met the reinforcements at Trefgarne, eight miles south from Fishguard, sometime after one o'clock in the afternoon. Cawdor and Colby were surprised to see him, and it was there that Knox tried to pull rank. Cawdor wrote a few days later to the Home Secretary, the Duke of Portland, that Knox had come under his command. However, another report of his goes into more detail about that meeting.

'Mister Knox halted the corps and came up to me with a paper in his hand desiring me to read it. I observed it was his commission as lieutenant-colonel which he observed entitled him to the command. I assured him I had no time to enter into the etiquette of military rank and only required from him an answer if it was his intention to give me his assistance and put the corps he commanded under my orders. After a short hesitation, he determined to put himself under my orders.'

Knox was engaged at a social function when the alarm came to him. So unless he rode back home to acquire his commission, there wasn't time for him to get that document, so he must have had it on him when he went to the party. Papers to flash at fellow guests? How self-important. (That is why I wrote that bit into the story.)

By five o'clock, the force had arrived within a mile of Fishguard and Cawdor, showing that he was not experienced in warfare, decided to advance towards the enemy in the dark.

The men, dragging their cannons with them, marched up the constricted and twisting Trefwrgi road, with its high hedges, towards the French position on Carngelli. There was no fight as written in the story, but a French advance party, under *Lieutenant* St Leger, had prepared an ambush. Volleys of musketry poured into the tightly compressed column at point-blank range would have resulted in heavy casualties for the British. However, Captain Nisbett suspected or understood how devastating this would be, advised Cawdor and he agreed to withdraw the troops to Fishguard. I believe that Nisbett's actions saved a lot of lives. The senior officers were billeted in the house, which is today the Royal Oak Inn.

By now, Tate's fortunes had changed. Many of his foraging parties had resorted to pillaging the local farms. One group broke into St Gwyndaf's Church to shelter from the cold and set about lighting a fire inside using the pews as firewood. The seventeenth-century Bible, translated into Welsh, was saved from the destruction and can be seen today in the fine little church. However, it is recorded that communion plate and silver was stolen by the invaders.

Discipline had broken down amongst the French irregulars; the eight hundred renegades, many of whom deserted to plunder and mutinous men threatened their officers. A Welsh girl, Mary Yates of Trelem, was raped, and another was assaulted and shot through the thigh whilst trying to escape. A supply of alcohol from a Portuguese wreck did cripple the ranks with drunkenness and morale plummeted when Castagnier's ships departed with obsolete orders to leave for Ireland to assist with the Bantry Bay raid.

9th March, HMS *St Fiorenzo* and HMS *Nymphe*, encountered *La Resistance*, which had been crippled by the adverse weather in the Irish Sea, along with *La Constance*. The British ships intercepted them and after a brief exchange both French ships surrendered. *La Resistance* was refitted and renamed *HMS Fisgard* and *La Constance* became HMS *Constance*. Castagnier, on board *Le Vengeance*, made it safely back to France.

On the evening of the 23rd, two French messengers arrived at The Royal Oak to negotiate a conditional surrender. Tate's terms written in the story are his exact words, but Cawdor bluffed that he had superior numbers at his command, which were increasing hourly, and he would only accept an unconditional surrender. He brazenly gave Tate the ultimatum of ten o'clock the following morning; otherwise, the French would be attacked.

In the morning, the British force was lined up for battle on the high ground overlooking Goodwick, reinforced by hundreds, perhaps thousands of onlookers, to await Tate's response. However, Cawdor had ridden to Trehowel Farm and received the American's formal surrender, although that document has subsequently been lost.

With no banners and drums beating, the French marched from the craggy heights and down to Goodwick beach, where they piled their weapons as ordered. At four o'clock, the prisoners were marched through Fishguard on their way to temporary imprisonment in Haverfordwest. It is said that many locals, particularly women, jeered and taunted the French by drawing a finger across their throat. The officers from the Legion were taken on horseback and later exchanged. After his surrender and brief imprisonment in Portsmouth, Tate was returned to France and was involved in bitter wrangling with the authorities. He is last mentioned in 1809, when he probably sailed back to America, and then disappears from history.

And that really was the end of the invasion.

Major Yates is an invention, but the notion that there were conspirators gives merit to two farmers who were hounded as traitors after the events. They were later found not guilty.

I have tried to stay true to history and include British men such as John Campbell, John Colby, William Edwardes, Thomas Nisbett, William Lloyd Davies, Thomas Knox, Stephen Longcroft, William Bowen and Dudley Ackland. Arthur Cadoc, a fictional character from *Marksman*, makes an appearance. I wanted to show the effects of the French landing, the very realisation that an enemy could threaten home and thus would inspire him to take up arms and march against them. After all, many boys and men had the same sentiment.

De Marin did not exist, but Le Brun, a Royalist, was second in command of the Legion and was one of the officers to hasten Tate to surrender. The other French officer's mentioned in *Tempest* did serve the Legion.

There is one person I have not written about, and that is Jemima Nicholas. She was a cobbler's wife, large and tall, known as 'Jemima Fawr' (Big Jemima) and became something of a heroine after the event. The story goes that she armed herself with a pitchfork, went out single-handedly into the fields and rounded up a dozen French soldiers. She convinced them to return with her to Fishguard, where she locked them inside St. Mary's Church under guard. She has spawned a reputation, earning the name 'Jemima the Great', and a deluge of literature in both English and Welsh has been written about her since.

By the end of the nineteenth century, the story had been exaggerated. Jemima had become a commander of a corps of women, sent out to deceive the French by pretending to be British soldiers on the hills. The Welsh female traditional dress of a tall black hat and red shawl fired the imagination of such a thing, but there is no actual proof that women were used to that effect. Cawdor never mentioned it in his despatches, and he wrote that Captain Davies was ordered to *'dispose the column to give the impression of greater numbers, which he did to great effect'*. This may be where the myth originated from and where the locals, including the women in their dress, watched the French surrender from the high ground.

It is also said that Jemima was awarded an annual pension for life. Unfortunately, there is no record of such a grant, although the widows of those killed by the French and others who were wounded received pensions. A memorial stone to her was erected in 1897 as part of the centenary celebrations. It still stands today near the entrance of Saint Mary's churchyard.

John Mortimer (younger than I depicted) was the owner of Trehowel Farm, claimed compensation for the damage done to his property of £133, ten shillings and six pence. In 2016, that figure is over twelve thousand pounds.

Cawdor, Knox and various other men received royal gratitude from George III and countless local honours. However, whispers spread of Knox, accusing him of cowardice and poor judgment. He was forced to resign as colonel and eventually challenged Cawdor to a duel. Diaries and journals are sketchy, and this was probably not fought. I think Knox knew his limitations as an officer, having asked veteran Captain Nisbett to take command and scout the high ground. But he panicked and then made enemies by arrogantly trying to usurp command.

In 1853, amidst fears of another invasion by the French, Lord Palmerston, who was the Home Secretary, bestowed upon the Pembroke Yeomanry Cavalry the battle honour *'Fishguard'*. This regiment has the strange honour of being the only regiment in the British Army, regular or territorial, that bears a battle honour for an engagement on British soil. It is indeed odd because there was no actual battle. The Cardiganshire Militia, marching up with Cawdor's force, did not receive the honour because they had been converted to the Royal Cardiganshire Rifle Corps in 1812 and carried no Colours.

The invasion is often written about as a drunken farce, a comedic episode that is not taken very seriously. But to the British people in 1797, the threat was very real, and it proved, without any doubt, that France could invade.

I would recommend anyone interested in this chapter of British history to visit the area. Pembrokeshire, especially along the coastal path, is simply stunning. Goodwick and Fishguard are subsequently larger but well worth visiting the harbours, the beach where the French piled their muskets and a walk over the headland to the fort. There is not much left now, just wind-battered walls, but the naval cannon remain, and you can get a clear picture of the surrounding waters and land. The Royal Oak, that was Meyler's house in Fishguard, has some interesting items on the walls. Inside the town hall, you can view the thirty-metre-long tapestry that tells the story of the invasion, analogous to the famous Bayeux Tapestry. Do also visit Llanwnda, which will give you a clear perspective of the surrounding terrain, Garnwnda with the cromlech (the peninsula has a number of them) that Mullone evaded the French in, Carngelli high ground, and nearby is a patch of land called Frenchman's Field, where it is said one of the invaders was killed and buried there. It's also worth visiting Aber Felin where the Black Legion rowed off Carreg Wastad Point to the cove to begin their landing.

I'd like to thank Jenny Q for her editorial work and jacket cover design. Thanks to Jacqui Reiter for her help with the French language. I am grateful to beta readers: Ian Langham, Jennifer Moore, J.G. Harlond, Margaret Muir and Michael Shankland who provided some very insightful considerations.

Much thanks must go to modellers and war-gamers Martin Small and Mark Davies, who brought the figures of the invasion to life and solved discrepancies regarding uniforms and historical detail. Their work can be downloaded from the internet as a pdf and is entitled, *The Battle of Fishguard, Units and Characters*. Richard Rose wrote the brilliant and very educational *The French at Fishguard: Fact, Fiction and Folklore*. I would also recommend reading Jenny Uglow's *In These Times*, a wonderful, richly informative book about living in Britain through Napoleon's wars 1793-1815.

David Cook
March, 2016
Hampshire

If you'd like to connect you can find me here:

@davidcookauthor
www.facebook.com/davidcookauthor
http://davidcookauthor.blogspot.co.uk/
http://thewolfshead.tumblr.com